P9-DEI-383

Fargo woke up and grabbed his gun

A silhouette of a man in the tallest western hat he'd ever seen. Too bad the man wasn't as slick as his hat. He came creaking in on cowboy boots with all the grace of an elephant turned ballerina. Always in sight thanks to the flickering sconce in the hall.

The intruder's eyes obviously hadn't adjusted to the darkness yet. Fargo stepped out of the gloom and slapped the barrel of his Colt across the face of the startled, blinking man. Fargo swatted the man around for a time, hitting him on the jaw, knocking the wind out of him with a punch delivered straight to his sternum. He finished by taking the man's fancy new six-shooter from him.

He was just busy enough that his mind didn't register the other sound in the room. By the time he started to turn, it was too late. . . .

THE TRAILSMAN
#263

ARKANSAS ASSAULT

by

Jon Sharpe

A SIGNET BOOK

SIGNET
Published by New American Library, a division of
Penguin Group (USA) Inc., 375 Hudson Street,
New York, New York 10014, U.S.A.
Penguin Books Ltd, 80 Strand,
London WC2R 0RL, England
Penguin Books Australia Ltd, 250 Camberwell Road,
Camberwell, Victoria 3124, Australia
Penguin Books Canada Ltd, 10 Alcorn Avenue,
Toronto, Ontario, Canada M4V 3B2
Penguin Books (N.Z.) Ltd, Cnr Rosedale and Airborne Roads,
Albany, Auckland 1310, New Zealand

Penguin Books Ltd, Registered Offices:
80 Strand, London WC2R 0RL, England

First published by Signet, an imprint of New American Library,
a division of Penguin Group (USA) Inc.

First Printing, September 2003
10 9 8 7 6 5 4 3 2 1

The first chapter of this book previously appeared in *Badland Bloodbath,* the
two hundred sixty-second volume in this series.

Copyright © Jon Sharpe, 2003
All rights reserved

Ⓟ REGISTERED TRADEMARK—MARCA REGISTRADA

Printed in the United States of America

Without limiting the rights under copyright reserved above, no part of this publi-
cation may be reproduced, stored in or introduced into a retrieval system, or
transmitted, in any form, or by any means (electronic, mechanical, photocopying,
recording, or otherwise), without the prior written permission of both the copyright owner and the above publisher of this book.

PUBLISHER'S NOTE
This is a work of fiction. Names, characters, places, and incidents either are the
product of the author's imagination or are used fictitiously, and any resemblance
to actual persons, living or dead, events, or locales is entirely coincidental.

BOOKS ARE AVAILABLE AT QUANTITY DISCOUNTS WHEN USED TO PROMOTE PROD-
UCTS OR SERVICES. FOR INFORMATION PLEASE WRITE TO PREMIUM MARKETING DIVI-
SION, PENGUIN GROUP (USA) INC., 375 HUDSON STREET, NEW YORK, NEW YORK 10014.

If you purchased this book without a cover you should be aware that this book
is stolen property. It was reported as "unsold and destroyed" to the publisher
and neither the author nor the publisher has received any payment for this
"stripped book."

The scanning, uploading and distribution of this book via the Internet or via any
other means without the permission of the publisher is illegal and punishable by
law. Please purchase only authorized electronic editions, and do not participate
in or encourage electronic piracy of copyrighted materials. Your support of the
author's rights is appreciated.

The Trailsman

Beginnings . . . they bend the tree and they mark the man. Skye Fargo was born when he was eighteen. Terror was his midwife, vengeance his first cry. Killing spawned Skye Fargo, ruthless, cold-blooded murder. Out of the acrid smoke of gunpowder still hanging in the air, he rose, cried out a promise never forgotten.

The Trailsman they began to call him all across the West: searcher, scout, hunter, the man who could see where others only looked, his skills for hire but not his soul, the man who lived each day to the fullest, yet trailed each tomorrow. Skye Fargo, the Trailsman, the seeker who could take the wildness of a land and the wanting of a woman and make them his own.

Tillman, Arkansas, 1858—
A madman's lust for sex and murder
of the most twisted kind.

1

Fargo eased his big Ovaro stallion behind a copse of pine trees and started watching the stage road with the lake-blue eyes that had seen so much in his lifetime.

He was used to bounty hunters trailing him. Fargo had helped out enough people in his days to amass a fair share of enemies. And these enemies included several crooked lawmen. Because they were afraid to face him down themselves, they put out WANTED posters and slapped some mighty big rewards on them.

So every once in a while a bounty hunter keen on earning a rep for being the one who killed the Trailsman showed up out of nowhere. Sure, the money was a factor but so was the prestige of bringing down Skye Fargo.

Such an opportunist—a gunny and sometimes bounty hunter named Jeb Adams—had been following him for three days and nights now. Fargo hadn't paid him much attention at first. Every time he hit a town, Fargo managed to find a place to sleep where Adams couldn't get him. Not that Fargo took stupid chances. He slept on his back, his Colt and his Henry right beside him in case Adams got lucky and came crawling into the room in the middle of the night.

But last night Adams had done something that turned Skye Fargo into a mortal enemy. He'd tried to poison Fargo's stallion.

Only the quick thinking of the old black man who slept in the livery at night saved Fargo's horse. The old man had awakened to the sounds of Adams—not exactly a graceful man—sneaking into the livery, then watched from the shadows as Adams mixed a powdery substance into the animal's feed bag that was brimming with oats.

The old man knew not to take Adams on. Adams would kill him in a flash. No, the old man wisely waited until Adams left, grabbed the feed bag, then waited until Skye Fargo showed up the next morning. He told Fargo what had happened and what the late-night visitor had looked like. Anybody who knew Fargo knew what his stallion meant to him. A wandering and solitary man like Fargo had few friends. It was only natural for his horse to become the best among them.

Fargo's first impulse was to find the sonofabitch and shoot him on the spot. The problem was, Fargo didn't know any of the local lawmen. Even if it was a fair fight, the sheriff here might decide that Fargo should be charged anyway. For a man whose only guiding light was the sun and the stars—he could go anywhere, anytime he wanted—the thought of prison, even for a few days, was the ugliest thought of all.

So Fargo decided to meet Adams outside the jurisdiction of the small Arkansas town he found himself in.

He made himself as obvious as he could this morning, taking an early breakfast at the local café, and loudly greeting the day crew at the livery as they arrived for work.

Two or three times, he spotted Adams glowering at him from various positions. He could imagine Adams's surprise and fury when he realized that the stallion was still alive.

Adams was doing everything Skye Fargo wanted him to.

It didn't take Adams long to show up either.

About ten minutes after Fargo had taken up his hiding place behind the pines, here came his good friend Adams.

The fierce Old Testament beard, the stained buckskins, the ancient and once-white hat, the blue glass eye glaring from the right socket, Adams was a hard man to mistake for any other. And that went not just for his physical appearance but for the way he did his business, too. He was well-known for not giving his bounty any chance to go peacefully. Many times, he broke in on them during the night and shot them in cold blood. Sometimes the wife and children of the wanted man had to watch the man die right in front of them. He'd even been accused, though not convicted, of raping some of the wives after killing off their menfolk.

One hell of a nice fella was Jeb Adams.

Fargo waited in the steamy midday heat wave—the temperature was on its way to one hundred degrees—swatting away mosquitoes, flies, bees, and other flying things he wasn't sure he'd ever laid eyes on before. Arkansas was one of the muggiest, hottest places he'd ever been.

Fargo waited until Adams passed him on the road. Then he quickly swung down from the stallion, grabbing his Sharps and stepping out onto the road so Adams could see him.

"That's far enough, Adams. Stop right there or I'll put three bullets in your back. The way you do with the men you hunt."

Adams was smart enough to stop his horse but not smart enough to keep his mouth shut. "Well, well, Skye Fargo. We finally meet up."

"You tried to poison my horse."

Adams, a huge man, had a huge and raspy laugh. "I believe I did, now that I think about it."

"I'm taking you in and having the sheriff arrest you."

This time, the laugh was even fuller, deeper. "I guess you haven't figured that town out yet, have you?"

"Turn toward me nice and slow with your hands up."

Adams did what Fargo demanded. When Fargo finally saw his face, he realized that the man was sneering at him.

"I said to put your hands up."

"I don't think you'd want to shoot me, Fargo."

"Yeah? Why not?"

The sneer widened. "Like I said, I don't think you figured out that town yet."

"Meaning what?"

"Meaning that the sheriff there is my cousin. Meaning that if anything happens to me, he's gonna come right after you. I told him who I was chasing. He said he'd help me get you if I'd split the reward money." The laugh again. And the almost luminous, somehow crazed, dark eyes staring at Fargo in the shadows cast by the brim of the hat. "But my cousin Bobby Wayne? He's just as mercenary as I am, Fargo. He'd help me get you all right—then he'd come up with some reason for killin' me. All nice and legal, you understand. And then he'd keep all that reward money for himself." He shook his head in mock grief. "Terrible thing when a man can't even trust his own cousin."

"Get down off your horse."

3

"Guess you didn't hear me about my cousin Bobby Wayne."

"I'm not worried about Bobby Wayne. I'm taking you to the next town on."

"That'd be Tillman, I think. They've got quite a Fourth of July celebration there, I'm told. In fact, that's where I'm headed now. Old friend of mine—did a lot of work for him in my time—he offered me a job. I'm thinkin' about takin' it. Thought I'd get some cash pulled together before I got there. That's where you came in, Fargo. You've got a nice price on your head."

"Down off the horse—after you pitch that six-gun and that rifle down here first."

Adams shook his head in mock grief again. "Awful thing that you don't trust me, Fargo."

Fargo used his Colt to put a bullet right through the highest point of Adams's battered, greasy old hat. The hat didn't sail off, just slanted to the right on Adams's large head.

"Nice shootin', Fargo."

"The Colt first. Then the Henry."

When Adams moved his right hand too quickly toward his holster, Fargo put another bullet close to him, about half an inch from Adams's gun hand. "Slow and easy, Adams. Don't give me any excuse to kill you. Because I'll take it."

"I was just doin' what you told me, Fargo." You couldn't see his sneer now but you could certainly hear it in his voice.

Fargo watched him carefully.

Adams slid the Colt from the holster, dangled it daintily by its handle, and then dropped it into the sun-baked dust of the road. He looked as if he'd been handling a piece of feces. Giving in to the Trailsman was obviously not good for the bounty hunter's pride.

"Now the rifle."

"You're a hard man, Fargo." Mocking him, of course.

"Just throw it down, Adams."

And then it happened.

Fargo had to give the man credit. He was able to drop the rifle to the dusty road with one hand while at the same time, with the other hand, draw a small revolver from the folds of his buckskin.

Adams got the first shot off, dropping from his horse an instant later.

Fargo threw himself to the ground. There wasn't time

4

to get back behind the pines. He rolled away from Adams's horse just as Adams started firing at him. Adams was down on one knee, getting his shots away from under the belly of his animal.

"Looks like I'm givin' the orders now, Fargo."

He clipped off two more shots, making Fargo roll behind some brush on the roadside. The tangled growth gave Fargo the only cover he could find. "Give up now, Adams. Go in peaceful."

"Hell, man, you're gonna be dead in a couple minutes. I'll be taking you in. To an undertaker."

Adams must have believed his own bragging because he now stepped out in front of his horse and aimed his six-shooter right at the brush where Fargo was hiding. He squeezed off his shot.

To a bystander, this moment would have looked awfully damned odd. Here it was Adams who'd done the shooting. But it was also Adams who, an instant later, clutched his chest as a flower-shaped redness appeared on the front of his buckskin shirt. And then he struck a pose like a bad dancer, his limbs all seeming to point in different directions. His small revolver tumbled from his hand, which, like the rest of his body, remained in this awkward position for another long moment. And then the huge man collapsed, the ground trembling as his body met it with real force and speed.

Not much doubt that Jeb Adams was dead.

Fargo had fired at the exact instant Adams had. Adams's gun made more noise than Fargo's, so an observer would have heard only Adams's shot. The difference between the two shots was that Fargo's had hit home, right in the heart. Adams's had gone wild.

Fargo picked himself up, dusted himself off, went over and hunched down next to the corpse. He checked wrist and neck pulse points to be sure the man was really dead.

Getting him up on his horse's back wasn't easy. It wasn't just the considerable weight. It was the form death had twisted Adams into. He was hard to get a hold of. But finally the Trailsman was able to carry him to the horse and throw him across the saddle. Fargo took a couple of deep breaths, and flicked away some gnats who'd been dining on his sweat.

He went through the dead man's saddlebags.

Adams had a couple of dozen WANTED posters. If the reward had been increased on a particular man, he'd noted that in pencil at the bottom of the poster. There was a notarized letter informing Adams that his divorce had gone through. According to a second letter in the same envelope—a bitter letter from Adams's ex-wife—Adams had been a terrible husband, a worse father, and a man who had embarrassed and humiliated her in every way possible, including a "tryst" with a woman down the street. The letter was from St. Louis and was two years old.

There was another letter from a man named Noah Tillman. It read:

> I hope this finds you well, Jeb. Though I'm troubled by a damned skin rash from time to time, I'm doing pretty well. My empire is making more money than ever. I say this knowing that it sounds as if I'm bragging. But hell, it's the truth. And you helped make it that way. Those two "eliminations" you did for me were important.
>
> You were also helpful in setting up my little project on Skeleton Key. That's why I'm sending you this letter. I hope you'll be able to join me this July 4th. I'll take you to the Key and show you how to have some real fun.
>
> I don't think there's anything like it in these United States, In fact, I'm sure there isn't.
>
> I hope to see you then.

The brief letter told Fargo that Adams had been doing two jobs at once—tracking Fargo and traveling to his rich friend's place. The word "eliminations" clued Fargo in that Jeb Adams had probably been a hired killer as well as a bounty hunter. This Noah Tillman had apparently been a customer. Rich men frequently needed to have business rivals killed. Hired killing was a lucrative business if you were good at it. And Fargo didn't doubt that Adams had been *damned* good at it.

Fargo jammed the letter from Noah Tillman in his pocket. He'd have a surprise for this Noah Tillman. Jeb Adams was going to show up, all right.

Dead.

2

Tillman, Arkansas was bigger than Fargo had expected. Thirty-five hundred souls resided here according to the WELCOME sign on the north edge of town. A clean blue river, new, if modest, homes, two full blocks of merchant buildings, two churches, a schoolhouse, and a courthouse lent the town an air of prosperity and friendliness.

The folks here knew how to celebrate the Fourth of July, too. Everywhere he looked, Fargo saw bunting and signs that proclaimed the special day. And the red, white, and blue colors weren't limited to storefronts and posters, either. Lots of folks wore red, white, and blue ribbons pinned to their shirt pockets. There was even an old swayback with a red, white, and blue blanket thrown over it.

Fargo naturally drew attention. A dead man is bound to attract almost as much attention as a naked lady. Kids, codgers, businessmen, farmers all paused in their activities to watch the rough-hewn man on the big stallion trail in another horse with a corpse slung across it. Even the short trip in the scorching sun had made Jeb Adams's body a mite smelly. Flies loved him. A couple of old people waved at him. He wasn't sure why. They probably weren't, either. They were just so used to waving—the custom of this friendly part of the country—that they did it out of habit.

Fargo didn't need to ask where the sheriff's office was. A wide, one-storied, whitewashed building had signs saying SHERIFF on both the side and the front. He lashed the reins of his stallion to a hitching post and walked inside.

He didn't have to do much explaining of the basic problem. A portly man wearing a leather vest that bore a deputy's badge was standing at a front window. He had quick,

7

friendly brown eyes. "Looks like you've attracted just about as many people as our parade will."

He put forth his hand and said, "Queeg is my name. Mike Queeg. I can take down all the information and off-load your friend out there. But the sheriff's in court right now, testifying in a case."

"His name is what?"

"Tillman. Same as the town."

"Let me guess. His father owns the town."

Queeg grinned. "You're half right. Noah owns the town all right. And that's only right. Whether you like him or not, he built this damned place. He cleared some of the land himself, that's how far back he goes. In fact, there's a painting of Noah in the courthouse. Shows him chopping down trees when he was in his early twenties."

"You said I was half right."

"Tom—he's the sheriff—he's the stepson. He was adopted after the fact."

"People like having the town boss's stepson as sheriff?"

"I know what you're saying, mister. But that isn't the way it works here. Tom ran for office fair and square. The first time, he lost, as a matter of fact. And Noah and Tom don't get along all that well. Noah expected Tom to do his bidding. But it hasn't worked out that way. Tom's a straight shooter with a real sense of right and wrong. He's even thrown some of Noah's hired hands in jail from time to time. They get out of hand, Tom doesn't treat them any different from anybody else. He may have Noah's name, but he makes it pretty obvious that there's no Tillman blood flowing through his veins." Then, "Say, you didn't tell me your name."

"Fargo."

"Fargo? Are you foolin' me? *Skye* Fargo? The Trailsman?"

"You going to arrest me? That's what the guy slung across his horse was trying to do. Somebody trumped up a murder charge against me in Wyoming. He was trying to collect on it. He was doing double duty, hoping to finish me off before he got to your town. Noah Tillman had sent him a letter inviting him."

Queeg whistled. "You sure got a way of comin' into a town, Fargo. You bring a dead man who's here because

8

Noah invited him." He smiled. "You should work for a circus. One of those advance fellas they send out to let everybody know the circus is coming. It's one hell of a way to introduce yourself." He nodded outside. "You know what his name was?"

"Jeb Adams."

Queeg's eyes and mouth narrowed. "He's been here before and he was a bad one. Couple of people got killed over some land Noah wanted. But Tom didn't follow up on it. I don't think he was scared to go after Noah. I think he just couldn't bring himself to believe that Noah could be behind two murders. He doesn't have any illusions about Noah—Noah does what Noah needs to, no holds barred—it's just that Noah and his wife took him in when he was only three. Tom just couldn't face up to what Noah had done."

"Was Adams around here long?"

"A month maybe. Raised a lot of hell here in town. Busted up one of the pleasure houses one night. Scared the hell out of all the girls. He was one mean sonofabitch."

"In the letter, Noah thanked him for helping out with something called 'Skeleton Key.' That mean anything to you?"

"It sure does, Fargo. That's the only other thing Tom won't look into where Noah's concerned." He hitched up his holster and said, "But let's get that body in here before it rots in that damned sun of ours. I'll tell you about Skeleton Key later."

Fargo spent a short time walking around the town and having himself another breakfast of steak, eggs, and potatoes. Banners inside and out proclaimed FOURTH OF JULY FEVER! A small marching band was practicing on a dusty side street. And boys and girls of every age set off firecrackers and sparklers. He even saw three or four ladies wearing dresses made up of the stars and stripes. They weren't kidding about having a "fever." It seemed to have infected damned near everybody in town, the way the streets were crowded with hometown folks and visitors alike.

Fargo had spent enough time in towns and cities to know when he was being followed. A lanky man in a dark three-piece suit, way too hot for this boiling day, had stayed on Fargo's trail ever since Fargo had left the café. Being that the only person he had talked to at any length was Queeg, Fargo wondered why the sheriff's department had found it necessary to put a tail on him.

He decided to have some fun with the lanky man. Fargo would walk real fast and then abruptly stop. He repeated this often enough to have the lanky man so out of sorts, he damned near walked past him. Once, Fargo ducked into an alley, hid in the shade of a blacksmith's shop, and watched as the lanky man hurried past, looking confused and frantic. Sure wouldn't want to go back to Queeg and tell him he'd managed to lose Fargo, now, would he?

A block later, Fargo was following the lanky man. When the man turned around, apparently sensing that Fargo was behind him. Fargo waved and smiled before taking off again, quick enough to shake the lanky man for good this time.

3

"I'm afraid I can't help you, sir."

This, or words like it, were spoken by room clerks in three of the hotels neighboring each other. Seems people in all the surrounding small towns came to Tillman for the Fourth. Every available room had already been rented.

At the next place, the clerk said, "This is on the top floor and ordinarily it's a storage room. But we fixed it up nice as we could 'cause we figured somebody'd probably take it."

"And that would be me." He paid the man and yawned again. He'd originally decided to ride straight through. But now he decided he needed some good sleep in a real bed before he started looking for the best place to cast his line.

Fargo carried his saddlebags up to the top floor, on the way pausing a couple of times to appreciate the loveliness of the women who were coming down the stairs. He remembered the livery man's remark about Tillman having a "higher class of women." Apparently the man hadn't been kidding.

Just before he entered his room, he saw a Mexican chambermaid, slight but fetching, watching him from down the hall. They exchanged smiles. He liked Mexicans, and while every group had its bad apples, he especially liked Mexican women.

The room was small but the bed was firm and the bedclothes clean. They'd fixed up a table with a wash basin, pitcher, and a couple of fresh towels. There was a spittoon, two ashtrays, a pile of magazines, and a pint of rye whiskey, this being some kind of reward for taking the room. There was also a window filled with blue sky—and somebody hiding in the closet.

The hider wasn't an experienced burglar. Made too much noise. Moved around way too much. But that, Fargo figured, didn't preclude the hider from having a gun and taking everything in Fargo's saddlebags. He felt sure that the hotel hadn't included the hider as the same sort of surprise the pint of rye had been.

"If you don't come out, I'm going to start pumping that door full of bullets," Fargo said. "All I want is some sleep. You come out with your hands above your head, I'll let you walk out of here and we'll call it square. If you don't come out right away, I'll start shooting. I get pretty ornery when I'm tired."

No response.

All of a sudden the hider was completely quiet. If he'd been like this when Fargo came in, Fargo never would've heard him.

Fargo raised his Colt, pointed it at the middle of the closet door. "I'll count back from five and then start shooting. Five, four—"

"No, wait, please don't."

Though the voice was muffled because of the door, there was no mistaking its gender nor—as the door was now flung open—the good looks of the buxom young woman who'd been crouching inside.

She was a burst of blondness and bosom, a tall, full-bodied woman of twenty or so in a gingham dress with a scoop neckline that displayed her charms to eye-popping effect. "Would you have really shot me?"

"I'm afraid I would've."

"But I'm a woman."

"I didn't know that at the time," Fargo said.

"And I'm unarmed."

"Afraid I didn't know that, either."

"Oh, I forgot." And with that, she raised her arms above her head, only emphasizing the ample fullness of those ripe young breasts that seemed eager to pop free of their dress.

"You make a pretty picture," Fargo said.

"Thanks," the girl said. "I'm Daisy by the way." Then, her brow furrowing, "Are you one of them?"

"One of who?"

"One of the kidnappers."

Fargo laughed. "Miss, I'm real tired right now. And I don't know what you're talking about. What kidnappers?"

"They took Clem."

"And Clem is—?"

"My brother. We run off from the farm because our folks wouldn't let us come to the celebration here. And now he's been kidnapped." She yawned. "And I'm every bit as tired as you are, believe me. All I've done for the past twenty-four hours is look for my baby brother. I need a bed just as bad as you do." She nodded to it. "We could both fit in there, actually."

"Yeah, I suppose we could."

"And it'd be nice to get some shut-eye before it gets terrible hot."

"I guess you've got a point there."

She glared at him. "So are you going to invite me or not?"

He laughed. "Well, I always do try and be neighborly."

They actually slept for a short time, but Fargo—every inch of him—came awake when he felt long, silken fingers start to stroke his manhood into stiff attention. They must teach them well in the backwoods where he suspected this young woman came from. Because after her fingers were through teasing him, making him buck up and down like a wild bronc, she then applied an equally silken, moist mouth to his lance, teasing it with even more skill than her fingers had applied.

She paused only long enough to pull her light undergarment off and then she straddled him, pulling her legs far enough apart that he could penetrate her warm, wet depths as fully as possible. She was a stern mistress, her hips demanding his best thrusts again and again, favoring him from time to time with the rose-colored tips of her bountiful, farm girl breasts.

When she tumbled over to her back, Fargo began slower, longer strokes that made her breath come in tiny explosive gasps. He had his hands tight on her buttocks and every time he'd clench them tight she'd slam upwards against him, bringing him so far up inside her that she started smiling out of pure joy.

13

He held back so that he could roll her on her side and take her so that his hips slammed hard into the creamy magnificence of her young buttocks and he continued to pulse and pound his shaft deep into her womanhood. She gasped, groaned, and then let out a scream that would have been chilling under any other circumstances. Then he rode himself home, ravaging her mouth with his tongue while he propped himself up with one hand, and filled his other with her firm, sumptuous breast.

He was just pulling away from her when the door slammed inward.

Two of them. One white, one Mexican. Both with enough facial scars to qualify them as sideshow attractions. Both with double-barreled, sawed-off shotguns and Colts strapped gunny-style around their hips. The Mex kicked the door closed with his boot heel. They smelled of heat, sweat, beer. Their clothes showed no trail dust, meaning they were either local or had changed clothes recently. Fargo suspected the former. The Mex wore a red checkered shirt, Whitey a fancier blue one.

"They're the same men who were following me and my brother yesterday."

Fargo glanced at his Colt, on the floor within arm's reach.

"You don't look stupid, mister," Mex said, "don't act stupid. Time you got to your gun I'd have pumped both these barrels in you."

"What the hell do you want?" Fargo said, as Daisy started getting dressed.

Whitey walked deeper into the room, within a few steps of the bed. "Stand up, mister."

"You want a better look at me naked?" Fargo said, grinning.

"I'd rather have a better look at you dead," Whitey said. "And that's just what you'll be unless you do what I tell you."

Fargo took a last, long look at his Colt. He was still tired enough that he felt a dream-like quality around the edges. He finally got a room; a beautiful bountiful farm girl made herself wondrously available to him; and now two gunnys who look, smell, and talk like they mean business decide to bust everything up.

Whitey nodded to Mex. Mex obviously knew what the

14

nod meant. He went right for Daisy, grabbing her with one free hand and slamming her up against the wall. "You be a good girl and this won't hurt. If I have to slap you around, I'll do it real hard." He smiled. "But that's how you like it isn't it, Blondie? Real hard?"

"What're you going to do to me? Where's my brother Clem?"

Mex wasn't much for conversation. He set the sawed-off on the table and went to work. He had a tiny, brown glass bottle. He uncapped it and drained its contents into his handkerchief. "Now you just hold still and this'll go nice and easy for you."

"What is it?" Daisy said, clearly terrified. "It smells bad."

"This won't hurt you. Just hold still."

Fargo figured it was some variant of nitrous oxide. The stuff wasn't intended for surgical procedures. Some people actually liked the woozy experience of it and used it socially.

The Mex clamped the handkerchief over Daisy's nose and mouth. The effect wasn't quite immediate but close. Within a few minutes, she slumped forward into his waiting arms. He threw her over her shoulder with the ease of a farmer hoisting a fifty pound bag of potatoes.

"I'll take her down to the buckboard in the alley."

"The back way."

The Mex sneered. "You think I'm stupid? You think I'd take her down the front way, kinda show her off to every-body in the lobby?"

"Just get her the hell out of here."

The Mex left.

Fargo watched as the door closed—the rage of help-lessness making a frenzy of his senses—so he wasn't fully aware of what Whitey was up to.

Whitey slid a long blackjack from the back pocket of his butternuts and applied it with fury to the side of Fargo's head. He was damned good with it, and Fargo rewarded his skills by collapsing into a naked, vulnerable heap on the floor.

4

The first thing Fargo did when he regained consciousness was stagger to the wash basin. He filled it with water from the pitcher and then dumped the basin on his head.

He'd gathered himself well enough to check the time. Twenty minutes had passed. Whitey was some expert with that damned blackjack. He sat on the chair next to the basin, dug the makings out of his shirt pocket, and rolled himself a smoke.

He was dizzy, his eyes wouldn't focus right, and he had a head like a big lumber mill saw slowly working its way right through the center of his brain. He knew only one thing for sure. Somewhere, somehow he was going to meet up with Whitey again. And that when he did, he was gonna open the bastard's head up like a can of beans.

It took a few minutes before he could stand up without wanting to fall down. Once he was able to maintain his balance, he dressed quickly, dried off his hair, shaved, and left his room.

Queeg was sitting at the front desk working on some forms when Fargo walked in. He put his pencil down. "Back so soon, Mr. Fargo? Hope everything is all right."

"Was looking for the sheriff."

"I'm afraid he's in a town council meeting."

Fargo snapped, "Why'd you have me followed?"

Queeg seemed genuinely puzzled. "I don't know what you're talking about."

"The hell you don't. A beanpole of a fella. Blond hair, long face. Dark suit."

"Damn," Queeg said. He sounded upset.

"You saying he's not one of your men?"

"Oh, he's one of 'our' men all right. At least he pretends to be. His name is Buck Larson. He's Noah Tillman's spy in town here. He must've recognized Adams when you brought him in. I'm ashamed to say he's a deputy here. He had an excellent record as a lawman, so Tom hired him. What he didn't know at the time was that Noah'd get him. Noah uses him as his spy here. He reports everything that goes on in this office back to Noah."

"Why don't you fire him?"

"Tom's about ready to. Larson's worked in a couple of big cities so he's valuable to Tom. Knows a lot about modern police techniques and things like that. But Tom's getting tired of Noah knowing everything that's going on down here."

Fargo said, "I just had some trouble in my hotel room."

"What kind of trouble?"

Fargo told him.

Queeg listened, shaking his head every few minutes. When Fargo was finished, Queeg said, "Another name for the 'mystery list.'"

"What's the 'mystery list?'"

"The people who've been reported missing over the years. Always around the Fourth of July."

"This have anything to do with Skeleton Key?"

"Tom and I are pretty sure it does."

"You've looked into it?"

Queeg shrugged wide shoulders. "As I said earlier, there are a couple of things Tom doesn't want to know about. One of them's Skeleton Key."

"Maybe he'll have to now, with two new kidnappings on his hands."

"Yeah," Queeg said thoughtfully, "maybe it's time now to really find out what the hell's going on."

The door opened and Buck Larson came in. Shock showed on his face when he saw the Trailsman. But only for a moment. He was enough of a professional to hide his feelings promptly and well.

"Say, I hope you didn't think I was following you this afternoon," Larson said.

"Perish the thought," Fargo said.

Larson caught the sarcasm and smiled. "I mean, I could

17

see where you might think I was following you. But actually—"

"—actually, you were just making sure that I was having a good time and that the citizens of this fair burg were showing me the proper respect."

"Why, damned if that's not exactly, right, Mr. Fargo. *Exactly*. I just wanted to make sure that everybody here was friendly to you."

"They were very friendly," Fargo said, "except for the two men who came to my room and kidnapped the girl I happened to be with."

Queeg said, "You know anything about that, Buck?"

Larson looked trapped. "Why, uh, no. Why would I know something about a thing like that? If I'd known about it, Queeg, I'd be trying to find the girl right now."

The door burst open and Larson was spared from saying anything more for the moment. A youngster, sheathed in sweat and out of breath rushed in and asked, "Is it true?"

He'd barely finished getting the words out before the office was filled with more kids.

"Is what true?" Queeg said, amused with the kids.

"Is the Trailsman really in town?"

Queeg laughed. "Well, Tommy, he's not only in town. He's right in this very office."

And it was then that Tommy's gaze roved over to the big man with the lake-blue eyes.

"Holy horses," Tommy said. He looked at his friends. "This here man is the Trailsman. Is that true, mister?"

While Fargo was busy meeting his public—if only half the stories of his derring-do were true—Larson used the time to slip out of the office behind the boys.

Neither Fargo nor Queeg tried to stop him. By that time, Fargo had decided to do his own investigating. Friendly as Queeg seemed to be, Fargo was no longer sure if there was anybody in this whole town he could trust.

"Maybe I'll go talk to Noah Tillman sometime," Fargo said.

"If you do," Queeg smiled, "talk loud. He hates to admit it but he's real hard of hearing."

The slender black man in the work shirt and overalls took the feed bag off of Fargo's stallion and said, "You're in kind of a hurry." It was a statement, not a question.

The interior of the livery was three or four degrees cooler than outside. The lumber of the place—like the earthen floor and timber—were saturated with the sweet-sour odors of road apples and horse urine. Blue-tail flies gorged themselves on the freshest of the road apples.

"That I am." Fargo described the two men who'd kidnapped Daisy. "You seen anybody like that around?"

For an instant there was recognition in his eyes, but the man said, "Hard to say. Could be a lot of folks. So many here for the celebration tomorrow, I mean."

"You sure about that?"

After setting the feed bag on a hook and leading the stallion out of the stall, the livery man said, "There're three colored folks they let live right here in town, mister. The rest live up around the river bend. I'm one of the three they let have a nice little house right on the edge of town. They do right by me and my whole family. And I appreciate that."

Fargo heard what was being said. "Appreciate it enough to stay out of trouble is what you're saying."

"That's right, mister. And trouble means never getting involved with anybody who's got it in for old Noah."

"This involve Noah, does it?"

"I didn't say that, mister."

"All right, you didn't say it."

"What I did say is that you owe me for another day and night if you're comin' back here."

Fargo paid him.

As he was saddling his horse, Fargo heard several light steps behind him. The liveryman. "For the most part, this is a nice town. They say down South the colored aren't treated so well. But I went up North for a couple of weeks to visit my cousin and I'll tell you somethin'. I'm treated a lot better down here than he is up there. And that's the truth."

Fargo sensed that the man had something more to say but he stopped speaking and turned and walked away. "I wish you luck, mister."

"Thanks."

The liveryman grinned. "You understand why I can't tell you that I saw a wagon like the one you described headed north out of town?"

Fargo grinned back. "Yeah, I understand."

19

5

Having served as a scout for the U.S. Cavalry from time to time, Fargo could read trail with the best of them. In this case, he was following buckboard wheels, which was less difficult. Every wheel had a peculiarity to it. Some sort of mark that made it distinctive.

The alley behind a hotel is generally a busy place. There were a number of wagon wheel markings to read. Fargo took the one that had left the clearest impression and started following it. He tracked it out of the alley and into the street, where it remained the clearest impression. Meaning that this was the wagon that had been parked most recently behind the hotel most likely belonging to the kidnappers.

The wheel mark was easy enough to see among the others. It had picked up a small nail somewhere along the way, the weight of the wagon sufficient to embed the nail into the wooden wheel.

When he got to the dusty, baking street, Fargo found that the tracks led north, just as the liveryman had said.

Getting out of town wasn't easy. The main street was packed with people loading displays on flatbed wagons for the parade. The Tillman name was on virtually every one of them.

People were standing on some of the wagons. They were practicing for the parade tomorrow and were in costume. Their attire told the story of the great Tillman family, which Fargo found about as fascinating as watching ants scurry down a sidewalk for a couple of hours.

The pageant used six wagons for the entire boring story to be told. How the Tillmans—a fat man gussied up in fake mountain clothing—had first pioneered this land. How the Tillmans—a skinny man sporting a peace officer's badge the size of a baseball mitt—had brought law and order to this place that had once been a roost for robbers. How the Tillmans—a pregnant woman surrounded by four screaming three-year-olds—had brought civilization to the local Indians, as depicted by a white man with a walleye and some kind of red goop on his face. He wore a headband and a single feather. And three other equally spellbinding floats. Maybe the locals would find this sort of event fun. Fargo would prefer a lady, a bottle, and a nice firm bed.

Liz Turner wiped a sleeve across her classically beautiful face and fed more sheets into her Washington Hand Press, the same printing machine that she and her late husband had lugged across three states and two territories while looking for the right place to settle.

Tillman, Arkansas wasn't her ideal settling place but for the moment she didn't have any choice. One wintry morning two years ago, her husband, Richard, had been shot in the back while coming to work. He had been working on a story about the place Noah Tillman owned—and would let nobody but a few of his gunnys on to—Skeleton Key. Not even Sheriff Tom Tillman had been on Skeleton Key. Liz was more than a little prejudiced where Tom was concerned. She'd been carrying on a very secret affair with him for more than eight months.

She wanted to find her husband's killer, but for now, the day she needed to get the weekly *Clarion* out, there was no time to dote on her memories of Richard, or to follow up on the strange rumors about the island. There was just Henry, her fourteen-year-old apprentice, who alternated working the press and picking his nose, and herself. She spent the time feeding paper into the sturdy press and checking every fifth page as it was printed, making sure everything in the hand-set columns stayed where it belonged. The *Clarion* didn't have any of the sparkle or sizzle of the bigger town newspapers, but she took pride in how neat it looked.

She inhaled deeply of the scent of printer's ink. To her the odor was more satisfying than the sweetest perfume. She loved the newspaper business. She'd grown up an orphan on the streets of Baltimore, nothing more than an urchin. So many young ones like that died of disease or hunger or at the hands of perverts. Somehow, she had triumphed. Somehow.

She glanced at Henry. His finger was up his nose. He extricated it quickly and then wiped said finger on his corduroys.

"Henry," she said, "I'm just afraid you're going to get that finger permanently stuck up there someday."

Henry grinned. "My whole family picks like I do."

"Never invite me to one of your family reunions, Henry."

They were both laughing about that one when the front door opened and Mike "Red" Grogan came to the long front desk where they took orders for printing (printing jobs earned them a lot more than the newspaper) and advertisements. Red was a spoiled rich kid but unlike most of the spoiled rich kids around here, he wasn't a snob and he wasn't mean. He used any excuse to come in here and see Liz. Lord, he had this terrible crush on her. She knew that she was still attractive at age thirty-two. She had that pretty face and a shape that had held its shapeliness and she laughed in such a soft, gentle way that she could charm a drunken grizzly bear.

She just wished Mike was about fifteen years older. For her sake and his.

"Hi," he said, immediately blushing.

He almost never had a good excuse to visit the newspaper office. In fact, most of his excuses were embarrassingly bad, usually revolving around how we wanted to learn the newspaper business and be a journalist someday. Right. His father would send him east to school—his father had graduated from Dartmouth and never let you forget it—and then, like his old man, Mike would go into banking. The family owned fourteen banks in the state. By the time Mike took the reins, that number would probably be in the vicinity of twenty. Nobody sane would turn down a job like that to work and starve at a newspaper.

"I might have a story for you."

She had to admit, this surprised her. This was the first time he'd ever offered her a story lead. But before she got too excited, she had to remember that this was a kid who

22

practically swooned every time he saw her on the street. And who would say anything to justify stopping by the newspaper office.

"A story?"

He leaned forward to stage whisper his response. "Fella named Fargo over at the Royalton Hotel told me that two gunnys broke into his room and kidnapped a girl he was with."

She looked at him skeptically. "Now, did this really happen, Red?"

"It sure did. And not very long ago, either."

"And his name is Fargo."

"That's right. Big fella. Tough looking."

"I've heard of him," she said. "He's tough all right." Liz smiled. Couldn't help it. By anybody's standard, Mike here had brought her one hell of a good newspaper story. She reached over and patted his hand, knowing that he was probably going to faint if she held it there very long. "You may just become a reporter yet, Red."

6

On a sunny day like this, it was hard to imagine a more beautiful land than the Ozark Plateau. Ragged mountain tops gleaming in the light, deep forests filled with game, and streams that gleamed clean and pure, perfect for the fishing the Trailsman wanted to do.

The tracks remained clear, the impression of the wheel with the nail in it clear as a beacon, no matter how many other tracks tried to obscure it.

He'd gone maybe a mile down the red clay road, the land falling away here and there on the plateau to reveal deep gorges, when his hat went sailing off thanks to a bullet.

Fargo acted instinctively, and just in time to avoid the second bullet that immediately followed the first. He dropped down on the side of his horse so the shooter couldn't see his head or torso, reining the horse over to a copse of pine trees several yards off of the trail.

There he yanked his Sharps from its scabbard, rolled away from the horse to a point behind the pines, and jerked up to his feet so that he could return fire.

The shooter was good but not that good. He pumped several more shots at Fargo, each one nicking at the pine behind which the Trailsman hid. But none scored a bullseye.

The shooter was hiding behind his own copse of pines on the other side of the road. Fargo did a little shooting of his own. He wanted to force some return fire so he knew exactly where the shooter was. They could sit here all day firing at each other and not accomplish a damned thing.

Fargo wanted to know who the shooter was and what he wanted. Did he have anything to do with the kidnapping? If he didn't, what could he have against Fargo? The Trailsman hadn't really met anybody else except the livery man. Since the shooter didn't seemed inclined to decisive action, Fargo took it upon himself to bring this little adventure to a close.

He pitched himself back up on his stallion, loaded up his Sharps, and started riding hard directly toward the pines that hid the shooter. But he rode in an aggravating zigzag fashion. Aggravating to the shooter because it made Fargo harder to hit.

Fargo pumped bullet after bullet into the shooter's hiding place, making it difficult for the shooter to get off any clean shots of his own, unless he wanted to take the chance of standing up and taking a couple pieces of lead in his brain for his trouble.

The superb stallion responded magnificently. The zigzagging skill was something the stallion had taken to right away. He seemed to know instinctively how much this pleased his master.

A cry told the Trailsman that he'd hit his mark; a second cry told him that he'd not only wounded the shooter but maybe killed him, too.

Fargo ground-hitched his horse, jammed his Sharps back into its scabbard, pulled out his Colt, and set off in a crouch toward the pines.

The chatter of forest animals disturbed the silence while the sweet tang of pine scent filled the air. The jovial, masked faces of raccoons watched him from tree limbs. It would be nice to stop and appreciate all these wondrous natural gifts but for now the Trailsman couldn't afford to.

A groan, human. The shooter. Not dead. Not yet. But he sounded very weak. Could be a ruse to draw Fargo closer but somehow Fargo didn't think so. That moan revealed not only pain but fear of imminent death.

Fargo continued to sweep around the deep stand of pines so that he could come up behind the shooter.

The moan again. But it was more resolute this time. The shooter sounded near death.

Fargo took no chances.

He finished the rest of his attack with a few stealthy steps that brought him to two slanted pines beyond which he could see the colors of a man's shirt. Red; checkered. The Mexican who'd been in his hotel room.

He came up behind the man but saw instantly that there was nothing to worry about now. The man was dead. Fargo had hit him twice in the chest.

Fargo made sure. He hunched down next to the man, raising a limp arm to check for a pulse. Nothing. No distant throb of a pulse in the neck, either. Fargo folded the man's arms over his stomach, the way the undertaker would when it came time to bury him.

He stood up and that was when he saw the dog. Lonesome old boy, some kind of mixture of hound breeds. Nose to something he was sniffing with great interest.

When Fargo went over to take a look he saw the Mexican's horse and a short shovel handle jammed into one of the saddlebags. What the hell would a man pack a shovel for?

The hound glanced up at Fargo with the old, sad eyes so common to its lineage. It moved aside as Fargo walked closer to check things out.

Not too hard to figure out what had happened here. The girl named Daisy most likely lay in the shallow grave of red clay that stretched before him. He went back to the Mexican's horse, grabbed the shovel and went to work. The earth, being freshly dug, and the grave being only quite shallow, Fargo didn't have any trouble.

Pennies on the eyes. Her clothes intact. At least she didn't appear to have been raped. One bullet in the forehead. Hadn't been dead long. The bluish tinting of her pale skin just starting.

He got the bed roll from his stallion, laid the blanket out, and then went and got the girl. Hard to believe she'd been a passionate, intelligent woman just a short time ago. She'd so desperately wanted to find her brother Clem. She'd died not knowing what had become of him.

The questions he'd had in the hotel room came back. Who was the Mexican exactly? And Whitey? And what did they have to do with the disappearance of Daisy's brother? And now, what made it necessary to kill her?

He rolled her up in the blanket, roped the blanket tight, and set it across the back of the horse. The top of her head and her ankles and feet stuck out of either end of the blanket roll. He held the reins with one hand and held the body down with the other. It was important to keep her from falling off. That was the least he could do to show his respect.

This time, the population of the town increasing with every minute because of the celebration tomorrow, Fargo had a huge audience for his entrance.

What man, woman, or child could resist watching a man on horseback bringing a dead woman into town? He had her covered from midnose down to dangling feet. But the blond hair and shapely ankles revealed that she'd been an attractive young woman.

He had to stop at several points so the crowd could part and let him pass through. Some people were offended, of course. A few others laughed, thinking this was part of some show. Dead young blondes apparently made for great comedy material. The kids, inevitably, were both scared and spellbound. They watched with solemn little eyes. For some, it was an introduction to death. Ducks died and cows died and horses died. But they'd never before seen a dead person. And for other kids, the dead blonde was a reminder of death they knew only too well—Mom dead of bad milk or Dad dead of a horse that fell on him, or a wee one dead of diphtheria.

He rode right up to the sheriff's office, swung down and went inside.

Larson was in the front office alone sipping a cup of coffee and smoking a cigarette. "Where's Tillman?"

"What're you so hot about?"

"You heard me."

"He's having lunch with the mayor."

"Does he ever do any actual work?"

Larson smiled. "Why don't you ask him that yourself?"

"Just tell me where I can find him."

"Over at the Roundup. It's the nicest restaurant in town. They brought the night cook in all the way from Little Rock."

"Good for them. Where do I find this place?"

Larson said, "You could always ask one of our helpful citizens."

Fargo was suddenly sick of Larson. "Just tell me where the hell I find this Roundup place. Or you'll be buying yourself some new teeth pretty soon."

It was clear that Larson realized that he'd pushed Fargo as far as he could. Now he was on dangerous ground.

"What's the trouble this time, Fargo?"

"None of your business."

"Sure, it's my business. I'm a lawman."

"Not from what I hear."

"That supposed to mean something?"

"It means that if you don't tell me what I want to know, I'm going to come over this desk and do a whole lot of damage to that smug face of yours."

Larson obviously decided it would be a good idea to tell Fargo what he wanted to know.

Fargo learned that you attracted even more attention when the dead young blonde was slung over your shoulder than when she was slung over your horse. You could get through crowds quick—amazing how fast people stepped away when they saw you were carrying a corpse—but there was more crowd to get through because everybody wanted to gawk.

She was starting to smell a little. He felt sorry for her all over again. This was how everybody ended up eventually but her time should have been a long ways off.

"She dead?" a man asked him.

"Just real tired," Fargo told him.

A little ways down the street, a woman laughed at him and said, "Bring her to the dance tonight. If you can sober her up in time. You musta given her a snootful."

"Yeah," he said, "she's gonna have some hangover, all right."

When Fargo arrived at the Roundup, there was a greeter right inside the door, an elderly fellow with a suit that hadn't fit him in twenty years and a pair of store-boughts that clacked every time he spoke.

"Good afternoon," the greeter said, trying to sound citified. "Would you like a table, sir?"

"I need to find Sheriff Tillman."

The man shook his head instantly. "You can't bring that—body in here. It'll make people lose their appetites."

Remembering what Tillman looked like from the photograph in the sheriff's office, Fargo pushed past the greeter and entered a large room with maybe fifteen tables where very well-dressed men and women dined and chatted and laughed in what appeared to be reasonably civilized circumstances. The flocked wallpaper, the two waiters in monkey suits, and the carpeting impressed Fargo, despite his sour mood.

But he wasn't here as a restaurant critic.

Tillman wasn't difficult to pick out. Balding man in a dark, expensive, three-piece suit with a full beard and a squat, but powerful-looking, body. The mayor was a scarecrow in a cheap suit, a brocaded vest, and full head of greasy yellow hair. He looked like a pitifully unsuccessful riverboat gambler.

Everybody was watching Fargo, of course, knowing at first glance what was inside the rolled blanket. He walked directly to Tillman's table and snapped, "Here you go, Tillman. You'll have to do a little work for once. Seems I've got this dead girl here."

And with that, he bent over and laid the blanket roll across the table.

Several women started screaming.

He wrapped her back up, slung her over his shoulder again, and said, "I'll see you in your office this afternoon."

Then he got the hell out of there.

7

Liz Turner pestered the desk clerk at the Royalton Hotel until he threatened to call Butch, an ex-con who served as both the handyman and a bouncer.

Liz said, "Butch wouldn't hurt a lady."

"Who says you're a lady?"

"Very funny. Where's the manager?"

"He's out of town."

"And he left you in charge?"

"That's right."

"I need to talk to that man for sure. He leaves you in charge and somebody gets kidnapped from one of your rooms, in broad daylight, and you say you don't know anything about it."

"You're making this up so you'll have a good story for your stinking paper."

"It makes a better story that you don't even know what's going on in your own hotel. A kidnapping and you don't know anything about it. That should make your guests feel real safe. Now take me up to that room."

Charlie Daly sighed. He was a master sigher. Very dramatic. His sigh told you more than you wanted to know about him—that he was weak, nervous, and easily given to pique, a word Liz had used in a newspaper story. Only once. Many readers complained that she was "showing off" with words like that. And you know what? Liz decided they were right. It had been a boring story to write and so she'd taken it out on her readers by using a word few of them would know. She'd never used such a word again.

The desk clerk led her up to the room. He sat primly on a straight-backed chair while she prowled the room. She and Charlie got along most of the time. But if Charlie felt that his job was in jeopardy, he'd get his back up and claw at you.

"What exactly are you looking for?" he said, sighing again.

"Don't go get your cravat in a whirl," she said. "I want to see if Red told me a whopper."

"Red? The kid?" He laughed. "My God, Liz, I don't have much respect for you so-called journalists, but I would've thought that you'd be more responsible than to listen to Red."

"I don't think Red would lie to me."

"Oh? Why not?"

She almost said, "Because he's smitten with me." Saying it, she'd sound vain and foolish. Was there any reason that Red would fib to her, even though he did have a crush on her? Maybe the fellow who told him was fibbing, just trying to stir up trouble.

She calmed down. "I'm sorry I insulted you."

"Me, too. For insulting you, I mean."

"I don't see much of anything wrong with this room."

"Nothing broken," he said.

"No blood," she said.

"Nothing missing."

"No notes left behind."

He sighed again. This time the sigh wasn't so dramatic. He said, "Believe me, if I heard a story about a kidnapping here, the first person I'd talk to would be you."

She sat down on the edge of the bed. "You know, this isn't the first time somebody's reported a kidnapping during the Fourth of July celebration."

"It isn't?"

"I went back through ten years of newspapers. This was way before we got here. Three times somebody came to the paper to report that somebody they knew had gone missing. They were sure it was foul play. You know, that the person hadn't just wandered away. The paper always ran the items in the 'Odds'N'Ends' column."

"Why not in the 'Law News' section?"

"I'm not sure. But it was strange."

Charlie thought a moment. "You know, before young Tom became sheriff and you folks took over the newspaper, Tillman decided what got in the paper and what didn't. Fellow that owned the newspaper was scared to death of making old Tillman mad at him."

"That makes me curious."

"Yeah? About what?"

"Well," she said, "if old man Tillman didn't want the full story in the paper, maybe he had something to do with those disappearances himself."

Fargo wanted to clean up and put on some fresh clothes. Hauling a dead person around left its traces on a fella.

He was just about to enter his room when he heard a quiet voice behind him say, "I was just about to clean up your room. My name is Maria Veldez."

The Mexican chambermaid he'd seen earlier. Couldn't have been more than five foot three, couldn't have weighed more than one hundred pounds, but her body was full and well-rounded and her face was beautiful.

"Well, don't let me stop you," Fargo said.

He used his key, opened the door, and allowed her to enter first.

"I was just going to change clothes," he said. He'd become almost painfully aware of her charms, couldn't think of much else, in fact. "You turn around and do your work. And I'll grab me a fresh shirt and pants."

She smiled. "This hotel is full of old men. I see them half-naked all the time. Big bellies and breasts like women and chins that nearly touch their chests." She sent him an openly admiring glance. "I wish I could see men like you walking around half-naked." She giggled sweetly. "Then I would have a good reason to come to work every day."

Fargo might not have been a deep thinker or particularly learned man but he sure as hell knew when a lady was expressing interest in his body.

He walked over to her and slid his arms over her shoulders and brought her to him. "I'll take my shirt off if you'll do the same."

She made a cute little face. Put a finger to her chin as if she were pondering philosophical problems. "Let me see. I'll have to think about that." Then she slid her arms around his waist and said, "OK, you talked me into it."

They were on the bed less than a minute later, as he teased the both of them by rubbing his rod against the soft sweet entrance to her sex. In moments they were both jerking and bucking, eager to get past this first stage. She eased him over on his back and licked her lips to the tip of his rigid manhood, flicking the head with her tongue, and then seeming to take the enormity of it completely inside her mouth.

He wondered if he could hold out. She was bringing him the sort of pleasure that blinded a man, made him one big erection, his entire body, his entire mind. Her tongue wrapped itself around his rod until—just at the moment he thought he could hold out no longer—she rolled over and guided him inside her.

The passion was reckless, two people flinging themselves at each other in a kind of carnal madness, him thrusting faster and deeper, faster and deeper, his hands clenching on her buttocks making her cry out each time he did so. Her breasts were wonderfully swollen with his tongue and her own desire.

"Now, Fargo! Now!" she whispered.

And he was glad to comply, sending his searing semen rich and deep into her.

Spent, they lay in each other's arms in the drifting ecstasy that always follows a good round of sex. Finally, he said, "Now, that's what I call getting my room cleaned."

"Yes," she smiled, "I'll have to remember your room number next time I'm in the mood to do a little cleaning myself."

Fargo was in need of a drink so he pushed through the bat-wings of a place called Curly's.

He wasn't surprised to find Deputy Sheriff Larson sitting at a table by himself with a fifth of whiskey in front of him. Fargo ordered a beer at the bar, and when he turned to look for somewhere to sit—not hard since the place was empty except for three old guys playing a card game Fargo had never heard of—Larson waved him over.

What the hell, Fargo thought.

The old farts gave him the once-over. One of them apparently knew who he was because he whispered through

33

a set of store-boughts the word "Fargo." Notoriety, he thought. All he wanted was a fishing pole, a fishing hole, and some sleep.

"I thought we might as well be friendly," Larson said when Fargo reached his table.

"Now why would you think a thing like that?"

Larson shrugged bony shoulders. Fargo had the impression that Larson was probably one of those bony gents who could be pretty tough when he needed to be.

"We're both working for the same thing, Mr. Fargo."

"Oh? What would that be?" Fargo had yet to sit down. He glanced around the saloon. It was new enough that the long pine bar still smelled of sawn lumber. The floor was dirt. But at least Curly's didn't smell of the usual vomit, blood, beer, and urine. But give it a year. It would have a scent like an old latrine.

Larson smiled. "Why, law and order, Mr. Fargo, law and order."

"Would that be law and order or Noah Tillman's law and order?"

This time, Larson laughed. "They couldn't be the same thing?"

"Probably not."

He flipped a chair around and sat with its back facing Larson.

"Tell me about Skeleton Key."

Larson shook his head as if he'd just heard a very sad tale. "So they've already gotten to you, huh, Mr. Fargo?"

"Who's 'they?' "

" 'They' are the ones who practice granny medicine and believe that half the women in town are secret witches."

"So there's nothing to it?"

"Is there anything to a witch on a broomstick flying across the moon?"

Fargo sipped his beer. On a boiling day like this one, beer was equal to the elixir of the gods. "Then why all this interest?"

"Because it's another way to get at Noah Tillman. Another rumor to ruin his reputation with."

"Then people don't really believe anything's going on out at Skeleton Key?"

"Some do. The ones I talked about. The ones who believe—as my mother did—that if you wrapped a rattlesnake around your throat, it'd heal your swollen tonsils. Fortunately, Papa would never let her try that particular medicine out on us kids."

"How about the other people?"

"Businessmen, mostly," Larson said. "There's no doubt that Noah runs this town. Hell, he should. He built it. If he hadn't been successful, nobody would ever have come here. You realize that?"

"I suppose that's right."

"But people get tired of being grateful. And they get tired of always having to kowtow to the most powerful man in the area. It's like the dukes and earls in England. Eventually, the serfs revolted."

"Anybody around here revolting yet?"

Larson poured himself a clean shot of whiskey—good bonded whiskey—and knocked it back without hesitation. "That's enough. The wife tells me two drinks a day and by God you don't want to go up against my wife. Ninety-seven pounds of pure hellishness when she wants to be." He said this with obvious affection.

"You didn't answer my question. Is anybody around here revolting against Noah Tillman?"

"Well, in quiet ways. Rumors, really. That's about all. That's their weapon of choice. They wouldn't dare go up against him directly. So they gossip. And gossip eventually takes its toll in small ways."

"So there's nothing going on at Skeleton Key?"

"You want an honest answer?"

"I'd appreciate it."

For the first time, Larson's face showed both strain and weariness. "I've got a very sick daughter, Mr. Fargo. A bad heart. I'm always taking her to Little Rock to see doctors. And I'm not rich. When Noah came to me and said that I was to report back to him on anything 'interesting' that went on in the sheriff's office, I said no. I said I like Tom too much. Tom's the best sheriff this town's ever had."

"I've heard that."

"Then Noah offered me money. I always thought I was an honest man. I took the money. Because of my daughter. Every penny goes to her. You can believe that or not but it's the truth."

Fargo surprised himself. He believed Larson.

"I did one more thing, too."

"What's that?"

"I told Tom what was going on. I told him that if there was anything he didn't want his old man to find out, not to tell me. I didn't want to cheat either of my bosses. I tell Noah everything I hear. But I don't hear much because I warned Tom ahead of time. He plays everything close to the vest. That leaves only one other person who could be supplying Noah with the information I don't have, Queeg."

"Queeg's a spy for Noah?"

He laughed and not without a certain respect. "That's Noah. He knew how much I liked Tom and he knew I'd tell him some things but not everything. So he put Queeg on the payroll, too. Queeg needs money like everybody else."

"Why doesn't he fire you?"

"Because anybody who worked for him, Noah would get to one way or the other. Tom'd end up firing everybody who ever pinned on a badge. If it's something real secret, Tom keeps it strictly to himself. Queeg learns some things I don't and vice versa. But there are things that only Tom knows about, too." This time his smile was tainted with embarrassment. "I guess I'm not the honest fella I always thought I was."

This was all supposed to work out so simple, Karl Ekert thought, as he looked down at the grave site that had briefly held Daisy's body.

Me and the Mex go into town, find the girl, take her, bring her back.

Easy as pie.

Except they hadn't counted on finding her in the room of some gunny called the Trailsman. And they sure hadn't thought the girl, after being knocked out with the drug splashed on the handkerchief, would suddenly wake up, jump down from the Mex's horse, and start running.

The Mex had caught her, wrestled with her and then, with rage, shot her in the forehead.

Somebody had returned the favor, Ekert thought as he looked down at the Mex.

Ekert looked at the ruins of their plan. The grave they'd

dug had been dug up again, small piles of red clay every-where. Plus the muddied shovel. And the body of Lopez itself.

The last time Ekert had seen Lopez alive was after they'd dug the grave. Ekert wanted to get back to the ranch so he told Lopez to finish up and then head back.

Then something happened. But what? How had anybody figured out that Lopez was here? Maybe Lopez, a man with a treacherous temper, had opened fire on somebody and started the whole thing that way? But who would unearth the girl and then steal her corpse? Whatever was going on here was very confusing.

He'd throw Lopez over his own horse and take him back and talk to the boss. Maybe the boss could help clear up the mystery.

Stupid damned Mex, he thought as he went over and dug his hands beneath the corpse. The flies were already feasting on the dead and bloody flesh.

He was beginning to think that maybe that damned gunny the girl had been with—he had something to do with this. Taking the corpse. Shooting the Mex.

Ekert frowned to himself. This was all supposed to work out so simple.

Fargo was on his way to the newspaper office when he saw a crippled man approach him. The man wore town clothes, a boiled white shirt, and trousers held up by suspenders. He wore a rakish hat at an angle. His gray mustache matched the gray hair beneath the hat.

"I'm Jefferson Tolan," the man said with a heavy drawl. "I'm the teacher at the school up the road."

"It's nice to meet you, Mr. Tolan. But I'm in a hurry, I'm afraid."

Tolan surprised him by producing money. A lot of it. Green money. Laid in the palm of his hand. "This is for you."

"Well, that's very nice. But I didn't do anything to earn it."

"That's the thing. I'm hoping you'll take the money now and then go about earning it later."

Fargo sighed. He wanted to get on and see the newspaper woman.

"I have a room right there in the hotel, Mr. Fargo. I want to show you some photographs of my little girls and see if you can help find them for me."

Fargo figured that it would take longer to talk his way out of this than to just go up, see the photographs of the little girls, and then say, no, he was sorry, he didn't have time for the job. Whatever it might be.

"All right, Mr. Tolan. But I've only got a few minutes."

"I appreciate this." He started to walk toward the hotel and then stopped. "Oh, I wasn't always gimped up like this, Mr. Fargo. I went looking for my little girls last year. One of the places I wanted to check out was Skeleton Key. But it seems Mr. Burgade had other ideas. Old Noah's had some pretty low characters working for him over the years, but they don't come any lower than Burgade. Anyway, I tried three or four times. The last time, Burgade put a bullet in my knee."

"You try and charge him with anything?"

"Wouldn't have done any good, Mr. Fargo. There're NO TRESPASSING signs posted all over. I was in violation of the law. He had every right to shoot me. I suppose he could've killed me and gotten away with it."

The hotel wasn't as well-appointed as the one Fargo was staying in, but the interior was constructed of good mahogany and the dining room they passed was scented with the aroma of good food well prepared.

Tolan had a room on the ground floor near the back. There was a monkish quality to it. The furnishings were dark wood, severe. Every wall had a bookcase. And no dime novels were to be found. Fargo wasn't sure who either Aristophanes or Cicero were but they both had leather-bound volumes on one of Tolan's shelves. All the other authors looked to be just as imposing. A globe sat on an end table while two walls were covered with historical timelines for America and Europe. A cut-glass decanter held some fair to middling grape wine that Tolan eagerly shared with Fargo.

Tolan went to a small rolltop desk and took two photographs from it. He walked over to Fargo and showed him the first one.

"They look like twins, those two girls in the pictures."

"That's what most people think. But they're not. Nancy's the eldest. This one. The other is Stephanie."

The "little" girls appeared to be in their midteens and gave every evidence of not having been "little" for several years. They were lovely but healthy girls with sunshine in their eyes and mischief on their smiling mouths.

"And here's what they looked like a year-and-a-half ago when they disappeared."

Fargo broke into a boyish grin as his eyes scanned the second photograph. "They sure aren't little any more."

"They turned out to be just as beautiful as their mother. She died when Nancy was seven. Cholera. I raised the girls myself. I damned near had to hire an army to keep the boys away."

They wore summer dresses that couldn't hide their strong, exhilarating bodies.

"I see what you mean."

Tolan limped over and sat down in a chair. "What I need, Mr. Fargo, is for somebody to get on that island and tell me if my girls are dead or alive."

"What makes you so sure they're there?"

"A woman from my church saw them talking to Burgade the evening they disappeared. That's all the evidence I need."

"Could they have run away?"

"No."

"You sound awful sure of that."

"I am, Mr. Fargo. The girls and I—we have a special bond. With their mother dead, I had to be both father and mother to them. They know what kind of heartbreak their running away would cause me. They'd never do that to me."

Fargo set the photos on the arm of the chair. "What makes you think I'd have any more luck getting on the island than you?"

"C'mon, Mr. Fargo. Don't be overly modest. I know who you are and what you've done with your life. If anybody could get on that island, it's you."

Fargo thought a moment. "Is there much river traffic in that area?"

"Some. Not what you'd call a lot."

"But people who know that part of the river?"

"Sure. Cap'n Billy is one of them. His real name is Harold Perkins. But he prefers Cap'n Billy.'"

Fargo smiled. "I can see why. And he does what?"

"Hauls things up and down the river for anybody who'll pay him. He even runs a kind of taxi service. There's a boat that comes three times a week. But if you're in a hurry and can't wait for the boat, you see Cap'n Billy. He's got an old tug boat. He works on it and lives on it. If you wanted to talk to him, you head two miles northeast of here. There's a long curve in the river and that's where you'll find Cap'n Billy."

"Well, since I'm beginning to get a feeling that I'm headed for Skeleton Key myself, I might as well look for your daughters while I'm there."

"Oh, thank you, Mr. Fargo. Now you take this money."

Fargo shook his head. "A young woman got killed earlier today. I owe it to her to find out what's going on here. This isn't for money."

"Will you at least have one more glass of wine?"

"I need a clear head. I'm going to pass." He stood up. "When and if I find anything, I'll let you know."

"You want to take one of those photos of my daughters?"

"I'm not likely to forget two gals who look like that, Mr. Tolan."

When he got downstairs, he found Queeg sitting in a chair under the overhang of a hotel. Old Noah sure kept Larson and Queeg busy, following people. He could see Queeg's eyes peering at him over the top of the newspaper he was pretending to read.

"Hot sitting on that porch, isn't it, Queeg?"

Queeg put down his paper, studied Fargo's face. "Larson told you, huh?" His cheeks gleamed with sweat. Fargo knew the feeling. His back, armpits, crotch, and feet were drenched in sweat, too.

"About you being on Noah's payroll just like him?" Fargo said.

"Yeah."

"You take turns, do you? He follows me a while and then you follow me a while?"

"I haven't given Noah anything for two days. Larson agreed to let me take it from here so I could have something for Noah. He likes you to tell him at least two things a day about the town. He always sends Manuel, his personal servant in, to get the information. Sometimes I have to make things up just to satisfy him."

"Well, how about this? I'm sure you've got more important things to do at the sheriff's office, so I'll just give you my plans for the next few hours. I plan to talk to Liz Turner over at the newspaper. And then I plan to go visit somebody named Cap'n Billy."

"If you go any place other than those two, will you tell me?"

"Does that include like buying myself a beer or taking a piss?"

"C'mon, Fargo, you know what I mean. I'm tryin' to set aside enough money so I can buy me and my family a little farm and get out of this business. It's just a matter of time before somebody shoots me. My wife has terrible dreams about it. Some gunny comes to town and I have to try and arrest him and he kills me. She always has the same dream. That's why I'm tryin' to set aside money. Noah's the only hope I've got."

Fargo laughed. "You tell Tom everything, too, the way Larson does?"

"Yeah."

"What'll Noah do if he ever finds out that you and Larson are playin' him like this?"

Queeg put a finger like a gun barrel to his head. His thumb was the trigger. "Then my wife won't have to worry about some gunny coming to town and killing me. I'll do it myself before Noah does it for me."

"Well, I hate to tell you this, Queeg, but I'm not sure yet where I'm going past this Cap'n Billy's place and even if I knew, I'm not sure I'd tell you."

"You wanna see a photograph of my sweet little kids, Fargo? That might change your mind."

"Seen enough pictures for one day."

"I could tell you about the farm I'm hopin' to buy."

"No, thanks. I already gave you your two things for the day. That's my part of the bargain. Now I want you to keep your end of it."

"I didn't know I *had* a part of this bargain."

"You sure do," Fargo said, his face showing sudden anger, his body suddenly taut. "You quit followin' me here and now or I push your face in for you. You understand me, Queeg?"

The anger was not for show. Fargo was sick of being tailed everywhere.

"Yeah, sure, Fargo," Queeg said, licking his lips, nervous now. The easy-going, amiable Fargo had been replaced by the Trailsman of legend. And the Trailsman, to be sure, was nobody to get riled up. "I won't be followin' you anymore, I promise."

The main street was so packed with day-before revelers that Fargo decided to get to the newspaper by walking the alleys.

He was halfway down the first alley, a friendly brown mutt bouncing along next to him, when the rifle shot came.

Fargo pitched himself away from the trajectory of the bullet, rolling quickly behind a line of small metal containers that held garbage. On this hot day, the stench was many times worse than it would normally be. Fargo didn't have any choice, though. There was somebody on the roof two doors down. The building sat between smaller buildings with lower roofs. Somebody who'd been keeping a close watch on Fargo. This was one hell of a town for people tailing you. He must have been near Fargo, seen that Fargo was going to turn into the alley, and quickly made his way to the store roof he was using.

Two more shots.

Fargo returned fire but realized that shooting back was useless. A man with a rifle on a roof had the clear advantage.

Fargo decided that the best thing he could do was work his way back to the head of the alley, get on the boardwalk, run through the building the shooter was using, and confront him on the roof. Find out who the hell he was and what the hell he wanted.

But Fargo would have to move fast. Once the shooter saw that Fargo meant to come at him, he was likely to take off.

Fargo had to duck half a dozen more bullets, a couple

of which came whistlingly close to hitting him, before he reached the head of the alley.

The shots had attracted a crowd and when he jumped to his feet, several men in Fourth of July duds said, "You all right, mister?"

But there was no time for reassurances.

Fargo worked his way to the haberdashery whose roof was being used. It wasn't easy going in the packed walls of humanity lining boardwalk and street alike. A dozen different perfumes and a dozen different tobaccos tinted the air with their scents.

Purty, purty clothes for purty, purty men, Fargo thought as he moved between the aisles of shirts, cravats, hats, and suits. Not his type of attire at all.

He was looking for the owner or a clerk to show him the door to the stairs. Even with all the noise outside, the store was unnaturally quiet.

He soon found the reason why.

A man in a very expensive shirt, cravat, and trousers lay face down near a door in the back room. Fargo's first impression was that the man was dead.

Fargo dropped to a knee, felt the man's throat and wrist for a pulse. A strong one. Then he saw the bloody gash in the back of the man's head where the shooter must have hit him. No wonder the man was still unconscious. He probably would be for some time.

Fargo nearly ripped the door at the top of the steps leading to the roof off its hinges. He was greeted by three quick shots.

Once again, Fargo had to dive for the ground—in this case, one hell of a hot roof—and roll away from the bullets. The roof was being repaired so there were stacks of construction materials here and there for both men to hide behind. The shooter was hidden behind a stack of two-by-fours very near the far edge of the roof.

Fargo chose a huge wooden barrel for shelter. He needed a moment to let his breath work its frantic way back to normal. He was breathing in gasps. That had been one hell of a run, from alley to roof.

He also took the time to peek around the barrel at exactly the same time the shooter was doing the same thing.

Fargo caught enough of a glimpse to know that his adversary was of Latin descent, either from Spain or South America. Not a Mexican. Fargo wasn't sure why this was his impression but it was. Even from this distance, Fargo could see that the man was middle-aged, handsome, and arrogant.

The man squeezed off two more quick shots.

As Fargo reloaded his Colt, he heard the shooter make his escape. He had jumped from this roof to a lower one next door.

Fargo, still cramming bullets into his gun, jerked up and ran across the boiling rooftop, knowing already that he was too late. The shooter had had the advantage of the rifle. He'd also had the advantage of knowing the town and its best escape routes.

Fargo peered over the edge of the roof.

He didn't see the shooter anywhere.

"Would you be Liz Turner?" Fargo asked.

"Why, yes," she said from behind the counter of her newspaper office. "How may I help you?"

Liz Turner turned out to be a fetching woman who had not quite reached her middle age. She was lovely of face, sumptuous of body, and blessed with the grace and poise of the true lady. True ladies didn't need money, expensive clothes, or a fancy family to possess all these gifts. Poise and grace were innate gifts and a simple woman could possess them just as readily as a princess. Liz Turner possessed them in ample measure.

"My name's Fargo, ma'am."

"Nice to meet you, Mr. Fargo."

"I wondered if I could ask you a few questions. If that would be possible."

Her smile was radiant. "Why, it certainly would be possible."

"What I'm looking for is some background on this sheriff of yours."

"Tom?" The way she blushed when she said his name surprised the Trailsman. He wondered instantly what her relationship with Tom Tillman was. "He's a good man. Decent. And very hardworking."

"Then he's nothing like his father?"

"Stepfather, you mean. And no, he's not. In fact—" She

hesitated. "In fact, he and his father don't get along very well. His father got Tom the sheriff's job and expected him to do whatever Noah wanted him to. But Tom's too honest. He did what was right, instead."

"So Tom Tillman wouldn't cover up a murder?"

"He certainly wouldn't."

"Your husband was murdered, ma'am. And I'm sorry about that. Has Tom Tillman been trying to find the killer?"

She leaned her elbows on the counter—a striking, sensual woman—and said, "You know a lot about me all of a sudden. Now I want to know a lot about you. Who you are and why all this interests you so much."

"I guess that sounds fair," the Trailsman said, and began to bring her up-to-date on some of his personal background. And on what had happened to Daisy and her brother.

8

The Tillman ranch was one of the places important East-
erners always visited when they were in this area of the
West. Noah Tillman—the man who'd created the ranch and
so many different business holdings even he wasn't sure
exactly what he owned—was one of those big, powerful,
quiet men who almost always avoided confrontation. He
had plenty of enemies who felt that he'd somehow cheated
them, mistreated them, bullied or bullshitted them.

He'd let you argue with him, pick a fight with him, even
curse him in front of his minions. Of course, if you actually
struck him, he'd likely lay you out. He'd been a bare-
knuckle boxer for a brief period in his youth. He still had
quick and deadly hands. But generally, he'd take any
amount of verbal guff you cared to give him and say nothing. Just walk away.

A week, a month, maybe even a year later, Noah Tillman
would express his displeasure. Not personally; not so you
could even prove he was involved. But there would come
a day when—after it was made sure that your family was
not inside—your nice new house was burned down. Or you
found your desperately needed line of credit at the bank
had suddenly vanished. Or you found one of your regular
visits to the local whorehouse resulting in a judge using you
as an example of the kind of hypocritical church-going family man who was actually a whoremonger—and you would
be forced to move and start all over again, shamed and
scapegoated by your community.

That was how Noah Tillman got you. And he reveled in
it. He knew you knew who was behind your sudden and

disastrous misfortune, and he was damned joyous that you knew.

The Tillman ranch had more acres, more good grass, more water, more beeves, more cowhands, and more house than any place outside the gaudiest mansions of Texas.

Noah Tillman sat in his study. There was a touch of the extravagant about the huge room—mullioned windows, parquet floor, chairs and couches of Spanish leather, rugs from Persia and China, floor-to-ceiling built-in bookcases, Noah being a well-read man—and a silence rarely broken. Noah never gave you much of his time, not even if you were an important personage. He found most conversations tedious and unrewarding. He spent most of his time reading books on the line of Caesars who both perpetuated and then ultimately destroyed Rome. He was especially interested in the games of the Colosseum, specifically the ones the Caesars created to honor themselves. He had accrued everything in his life. Now it was time to entertain himself in lavish and unique ways.

At the moment, he was not as impatient as usual. He had a real interest in what Ekert was telling him. He wasn't happy with Ekert—he was rarely happy with anybody—but he was disturbed by what he was hearing and so he listened carefully.

"But at least we've got the third one now," Ekert said. He was self-conscious sitting in such a fine leather chair. Sitting in front of a dangerous and completely incomprehensible white-haired gentleman with cruel, eagle-like features and dark eyes that seemed inhuman.

Tillman was always impeccably attired. Expensive, hand-made suits ordered half a dozen at a time from Chicago; the finest linen shirts and cravats; and French cuffs adorned with large 24 carat gold cuff links that bore the heads of the Caesars. It was easy to see that he was hard of hearing. Despite his imposing presence, he had to tilt his head to the right to hear well and even then he lost a good deal of what was said.

"You seem very satisfied with yourself," Tillman said.

"Well, things turned out all right."

"You think so?"

It was easy to sense that Noah Tillman wasn't going to

turn the other cheek in this particular moment. He was going to confront Ekert and Ekert was just now realizing it.

"I pay you three times what you made before you went to work with me."

"Yessir." Nervousness in Ekert's voice now.

"And when your mother was sick in Kansas last year, I let you take a full month off.

"And when your son took sick, I paid all the expenses at the Denver hospital."

"Yessir."

"I feel I've been loyal to you, Mr. Ekert." He had started to play with his left cuff link. To cover it with his thumb and then rub it, as if the rubbing would produce a magical occurrence—a secret door sliding open, a genie in cowboy get-up suddenly appearing.

"Yessir, you've been very loyal to me, Mr. Tillman."

"But now when I ask you to perform a simple task for me, you let me down."

"Sir, as I told you, we killed the girl so she won't be any trouble—"

"Yes, Mr. Ekert, you killed the girl all right. But that's not the end of it."

"It's not?"

Tillman made a displeased face and sat back in his baronial leather chair. "A few minutes ago you sat there looking so smug, I wanted to slap you across the face."

"I didn't mean to look smug, Mr. Tillman."

"Think, Ekert." Tillman tapped his right temple. "Think it through. You're not a stupid man."

"Thanks for saying that, sir."

"So sit there and think about it. There's unfinished business here, Mr. Ekert. Business that could bring this whole thing down."

"There is, sir?"

"Yes, Mr. Ekert. There is. Now I'm going to walk over there and get myself a brandy. And when I come back here, I want you to have your answer ready. All right?"

"Yessir."

Ekert did his best to smile but couldn't quite make it.

9

After Fargo told her about himself, Liz Turner told the Trailsman an interesting story, one that held elements of a late night campfire ghost tale.

Looking back through the *Clarion* files accumulated before she and her husband came to Tillman, she saw four stories over fourteen years that said basically the same thing. Eight travelers were reported missing over these years and the relatives of each one eventually ended up here in Tillman, insisting that their loved ones were last seen alive right here.

The funny thing was, Stan Tillman, Noah's cousin, who had been sheriff before Tom, claimed not to have known anything about the disappearances. When Liz had confronted him with these stories, Stan said that these loved ones had to blame somebody for their relatives vanishing. Family troubles of various kinds was why these folks had vanished of their own free will.

When they'd first come here, Liz and Richard had paid the Tillmans the same homage that everybody else did. They walked wide of writing any stories that were in any way critical of the family. The newspaper thrived. Noah Tillman personally saw to it. They accommodated him in every single public dispute, even at those times when Noah Tillman was clearly acting illegally and being a bully to get his way.

Until the incident with the card game.

One of Noah's nephews had played twelve beery hours of poker one night and lost a lot more money than he could afford. The man he lost it to was a friend of his. Or had been until this game. The nephew got so angry that the friend even offered to return his winnings. He valued the friendship too much to lose. But the nephew only scoffed. He didn't want money, he said. He just wanted a chance to win his money back. After half an hour of browbeating, the friend finally agreed to play double or nothing, though he accurately predicted what would happen.

The nephew would play double or nothing, highest card draw, and lose. Then he'd owe twice as much money. And demand that they play again. And all the friend wanted to do was quit and go home. He was tired. He had to work in the morning.

The nephew persisted. They went five times for double or nothing and the nephew lost every time. The entire saloon of early morning stragglers watched it all with grim humor. The barkeep tried to close up for the night but the nephew said he'd be sorry if he did. The barkeep didn't want to take on a Tillman. That was for sure.

The upshot of all this was that the friend was found in the morning with the back of his head smashed in and his money gone.

Most folks assumed that the nephew had followed the friend home and killed him on a deserted, moonlit road.

Wrong, according to Sheriff Stan Tillman.

What happened, he insisted, was that the friend had been drunk and had fallen off his horse backwards, thus injuring the back of his head.

There were any number of things wrong with this claim. There was no rock or boulder on the roadside to cause such damage. Even if there were, to fall off the horse in the way the lawman claimed would have been a highly unlikely fluke. Men falling from horses tend to go head first or sideways, rarely backwards. And the crushed skull itself had been pretty obviously done with a weapon or tool of some kind. Accidental injuries wouldn't have been as deftly and thoroughly placed. Or been inflicted several times.

All the good journalistic instincts of Liz and Richard Turner took over. They just couldn't let this one go by. They began interviewing people who'd been at the saloon that night. They walked through the entire episode as laid out by Sheriff Stan. Then they hired an out of town doc with a degree from back east to come to Tillman to investigate the whole matter. It was his conclusion that it was very unlikely that the friend had died in the manner Sheriff Stan insisted he did.

The Turners published their story. What was said wasn't as important as what *wasn't* said. While the story didn't come right out and say that the nephew, a notoriously sore loser, had killed his friend, you could certainly read the story that way.

And that was the way most *Clarion* readers chose to read it, too. For the first time the House of Tillman had been challenged. And everybody knew it.

The Turners had several great follow-up stories ready to go, each one more damning than the others about how Tillman law and order worked just fine for the Tillmans but not for anybody else.

But before they could go to press, the newspaper office was burned to the ground during the night.

And a night after that, their house was torched. They'd barely been able to escape.

Sheriff Stan was retired within two months. The Turners rebuilt their house and the newspaper office. And for a long time, clearly intimidated, they had nothing unfavorable to say about the Tillman empire. They were ashamed of themselves, but shame was better than death. And they had no doubt that old Noah would kill them if he saw a need to.

But when the story about the missing travelers came up—and they checked back through past newspapers—they became suspicious. Richard began investigating. And, not long after, was backshot and killed.

Liz finished her coffee and said, "And now there's the girl you found dead. And her missing brother."

"Sure fits in with the rest," Fargo said. "I'm not a journalist, but I've looked into a few murders in my time. And I'm sure going to look into this one."

"Any idea how you'll start?"

"I need to find the white man who came up to my room with the Mexican. And that means starting with getting the body and bringing it back here for identification."

She smiled. "I was going to say 'be careful,' the way women always do. But I have a feeling you'll be able to handle yourself just fine. But he's got a lot of rough men working for him, old Noah does. I'll talk to Tom about this. He'll be honest with me."

Fargo picked up his hat. "Any easy way into that ranch of Noah's?"

"Not unless you're awful lucky. He has dogs and men riding shotgun and standing sentry all over the land that surrounds the house itself. You could get on the property with no problem—just wait until one of the shotgun riders is working a different part of the spread—but getting into the house would be next to impossible."

"Maybe I'll try the easy way."

"I'm not sure there *is* an easy way, Fargo."

Fargo laughed. "It's called walking up to the front door and knocking and asking to see old Noah."

"I guess I never thought of that," she smiled. "That might just work. But even if they let you in, what would you say?"

Fargo said, "That's the part I haven't come up with yet."

"So," Noah Tillman said, returning to sit behind his desk and sip his brandy. "Have you figured out the part you left unfinished, Mr. Ekert?"

Tillman could imagine what was going through Ekert's mind. This was the ultimate final exam. Ekert had to know that if he failed to answer correctly, there would be hell to pay. And it would be a hell much more fiery than getting a simple "F" on a progress report. He had to know that Tillman would have two or three of his men take Ekert somewhere out of the county and kill him. He'd be buried so deep that he'd never be found. And everybody involved would proclaim with great dramatic innocence that they had no idea where Mr. Ekert had gone to.

Ekert smiled anxiously. "I'm almost afraid to answer, Mr. Tillman. If I said the wrong thing—"

"But you have to answer, Mr. Ekert."

"It's just so hot in here—" Ekert's face gleamed with sweat. Even his neck glistened with moisture. You could almost feel sorry for him.

"It'll be worse for you if you don't answer at all, Mr. Ekert. Let me assure you of that."

Ekert, obviously unable to deal with the tension anymore, blurted out, "Is it that I didn't kill Fargo?"

The silence was thunderous. It squeezed even more sweat

out of Ekert. And it made his entire head twitch, as if it might just rip free of his neck.

For a ham like old Noah, this was a moment to enjoy and extend. Maybe he could get Ekert to twitching like a chicken that had just been beheaded. Maybe Ekert would start running around the study, stumbling blindly into things and finally falling on the floor and going into spasms so severe, his spine would snap. Now that—for a man like Noah who wanted to amuse himself with new and novel situations—that would be something to see.

Ekert said, "Would you just please tell me if I answered right, Mr. Tillman?"

"Well, before I tell you, let me ask you if you want to change your answer."

Ah, genius. Another way of prolonging Ekert's suffering.

"You'd let me change it?"

"Yes, I would, Mr. Ekert."

"Does that mean that my answer was wrong, Mr. Tillman?"

"Not at all. It just means I'm in a generous mood and I'm willing to give you another try."

"If my answer was right, would you tell me now?"

"I will if you'd like me, too, Mr. Ekert. But if it's wrong, I wouldn't be able to give you that extra chance."

"Oh, God."

More brandy. "It's all up to you. I can tell you if your answer is right—or I can give you a second guess."

"I'll take a second guess." Ekert glanced around the study, as if the answer might be hidden somewhere in its appointments and furnishings.

"I'll give you two minutes."

Tillman took his watch from his vest pocket. "Ready, Mr. Ekert?"

"Ready."

The sweat glazed Ekert now. And the shaking and the twitching—spasms, real spasms now. Except for a man who was about to hang, Tillman had rarely seen anybody look so forlorn.

Ekert licked dry lips. Smiled anxiously up at Tillman. "I'm real nervous."

"You're wasting your time and mine, Mr. Ekert."

Once again, Ekert blurted his answer. "It's because I didn't kill Fargo."

"You're sure of that, Mr. Ekert? You're sure that's the answer I'm looking for?"

But Ekert didn't look sure at all. And he didn't need to tell this to Tillman, either.

Noah Tillman smiled. "You managed to give me the right answer, Mr. Ekert."

"I did?" He sounded shocked.

"Yes, now go clean yourself up, Mr. Ekert."

From the stain on the front of his pants, it was clear that Ekert had wet himself.

"And now that you know what I want you to do, I want it done right away."

"I understand that, Mr. Tillman. I'm sorry I didn't kill him this morning."

He walked bow-legged from the study. Tillman went over and opened a window. Some fresh air, even if the day was hot, torpid. Fresh air was what he needed.

10

Fargo had spent time on waters of various kinds. On wide creeks with Indian friends, on rivers working as a hand, even on the Pacific Ocean, though never far from the coast.

Cap'n Billy's tugboat brought back a lot of memories. It was a flat craft with the sheer—the top of the tug's sides—running only a foot high. The bow was open for loading and off-loading whatever Cap'n Billy was hiding. On a hot night like this, a myriad of acrid odors—the remnants of various things the Cap'n had hauled—kept the air sour. The sentimental sound of the squeezebox playing an old forlorn Irish sea ballad brought back Fargo's time on the water.

Fargo ground-hitched his stallion and walked down the hill leading to the riverside where a heavy rope lashed the tug to a large steel spike driven deep into an oak tree.

No cargo onboard tonight. Just an old man sitting on the empty deck with a dog lying next to his chair and a cat on his lap.

Cap'n Billy didn't stop playing but he did look up and say, "Sara Jane told me I was gonna have a visitor tonight."

Fargo boarded the craft and walked its length to where Cap'n Billy sat.

"Sara Jane is your daughter?"

"Nope. She's a witch."

"I see."

"I can tell by your tone you're not a believer."

"Not a believer, not an unbeliever. I could be convinced either way."

"Have a seat, stranger."

Fargo smiled. "I guess she didn't tell you my name, huh?"

The Captain quit playing. "See, there's that skeptic tone again. She ain't that advanced in her witchery yet."

"I see."

"She's my niece and she ain't but ten years old."

"Oh." Fargo knew that this wasn't going to be fun or fast. Here was an old man who loved to talk and ramble while he talked. And getting him to focus would take some work.

"Most witches don't get good 'til they get their menses."

"I guess I hadn't heard that one."

"That's 'cause you're like most people. You don't *want* to hear it. It scares ya to think about, that there's a whole world all around us—this invisible world—that really controls everything we do. But you'd rather not know about it because then you'd have to *do* somethin' about it. You'd have to start wearin' garlic to keep the vampires away, and keep a silver bullet to fend off the werewolves, and wear special amulets and crystals at special times of the year so the demons don't get you."

It crossed Fargo's mind that sitting out here with this old fart could get downright spooky if he let it. Just the river and the wild woods on both banks and a span of sky that seemed eerily alive with glowing stars. He half expected to see some lizard-like monster come up from the water.

"I actually came here to ask you about Skeleton Key."

"You stay away from Skeleton Key."

"How come?"

He was dressed in a soiled captain's hat and a ragged red shirt that had once had longer sleeves. Apparently he'd torn them off when the weather had turned hot. He had one glass eye, an earring dangling from his left lobe, and several holes where teeth had once resided. He set his squeezebox down and picked up a violently hairy gray cat and began to stroke her.

"The screams."

"The screams?" Fargo said.

"I've heard 'em."

"On Skeleton Key?"

"You bet on Skeleton Key."

"Anybody else hear these screams?"

"You don't take my word for it?"

"It's always better when you have two or three other witnesses."

"Well, for one, Queenie here heard 'em."

"The cat?"

"You damn betcha the cat. You got somethin' against cats?"

"No, nothing at all. It's just that Queenie might have a hard time *telling* me about the screams. If you see what I mean."

"Well, I can hear her just fine and dandy. She talks to me all the time. Don't you, Queenie?" At which point the cat looked up and lapped his chin with a long pink tongue. Hell, maybe they *did* communicate with each other.

"And she wasn't the only one who heard them screams." He nodded down to the sad-eyed beagle lying beside him. "Pirate Jack heard 'em, too. You said you wanted two or three witnesses. Well, you're lookin' at 'em, son. Me, Queenie, and Pirate Jack."

Fargo hesitated, taking in the soft aromas of weeping willows. Life on this tug boat—at least at night—could be comfortable and relaxing. As long as Cap'n Billy and his talking pets were far, far away.

"What I need to know, Cap'n Billy, is how I can get on that island."

"Ain't no way. Not with the dogs."

"What dogs?"

"I ain't actually seen 'em but I sure as hell have heard 'em. Man killers, for sure. Plus there's the timber itself. I played there when I was a young'un. Really easy to get lost. Thickest timber I ever seen. Like one of them African jungles you read about."

"I couldn't get past the dogs?"

"Not them dogs. The Key's good sized but not *that* good sized. Them dogs would find you right away. You'd be dead in two minutes."

Fargo set to rolling himself a smoke. He offered Cap'n Billy the makings but Billy shook his head. "What else is on the Key? You got any idea?"

"I got no idea. Not for sure. But I got suspicions."

"Like what?"

"Well, I was goin' by there one morning when it was

real foggy. Could barely see your own hand. If I didn't know this part of the river so well, I'd never have chanced it. Anyway, I got a little lost and got closer to the key than I normally would. They've got NO TRESPASSING signs everywhere and who knows if they wouldn't just start shootin' at somebody who got too close to them? Now I can't swear this because I could only see in little bits and pieces through the fog. But I'm pretty sure I saw what they was off-loadin' that day. And this was two days before the Fourth of July a couple of years ago."

"You didn't say what they were off-loading."

"Well, it looked to me like they was takin' bodies off and puttin' them on the key. The funny thing was, the little look I got at them, the bodies didn't seem dead. Their arms was flailin' around too much. They looked like they might justa been knocked out or somethin', you know what I mean? Kinda flounderin' around. But you'd never see a dead person flounder like that. I had a lotta experience with dead people, believe me."

He obviously wanted Fargo to ask him about all the experiences he'd had with dead people, but Fargo knew that he might be here for hours if he let the Cap'n start slinging the shit.

"You ever think of any way you could *sneak* on that island, Cap'n?"

The old fart laughed. "Sure. There's an easy way."

"There is?"

"Get yourself captured and let them *take* you there."

11

A few minutes later, Fargo was on the road to the Noah Tillman ranch. Given all the turbulence around him, Fargo realized that the deep shadows on either side of the road could hold people who wanted to get rid of him. The animals in the surrounding woods sounded lonely and desolate in the transition from day to night.

Soon enough, Fargo passed the spot on the stage road where Daisy had been buried. Her only sin had been being the missing man's sister. No matter where you went, there were predators like the Tillman family. And no matter where you went, there were innocent victims like Daisy. The primitive law of the jungle also applied to the affairs of human beings. He was most interested in meeting Noah Tillman. He just hoped he could hold his temper in check.

As he approached the Tillman ranch twenty minutes later, he noticed that a pine tree shook slightly, even though there was no wind at all. Man with a rifle, for sure, monitoring Fargo. And if there was one, then there'd be two.

The second one appeared moments later, stepping out from behind a pile of boulders off to the side road.

Even in the dusk, which tended to soften things, the gunny looked formidable. Short, wide, and looking very comfortable with the carbine he'd pointed right at Fargo.

"Private property here, mister."

"I was hoping to see Noah Tillman. Name's Fargo."

"Mr. Tillman only sees people by appointment. You got an appointment, mister?"

Fargo smiled. "Not so's you'd notice."

"Then head back to town."

"Which one of you's the better shot?"

"What the hell you talking about?"

"You or your friend in the tree?"

In answer to his question, the man in the tree fired three quick shots close enough to the big Ovaro stallion to make it mighty nervous.

"I'm sure neither you nor your horse really wants to find out which of us is the better shot, mister. Now head back to town."

With two Winchesters trained on him, Fargo knew there was no point in playing hero. He had no doubt that they were working up to killing him. Trespassing, they'd say. Tried to reason with him, they'd say. Then he went for his gun, they'd say. He didn't give us no choice, they'd say.

"And here I was hoping for a nice, friendly visit," Fargo said.

"You haul your ass back to town and right now, trouble-maker," said the man in the tree, a disembodied voice in the gathering gloom.

"Guess I don't have much choice, do I?" Fargo said to the gunny in front of him.

"You ain't got no choice at all, mister."

The best way to make sure they'd think he was heading back to town was to make one more try to see Noah Tillman.

"Would you at least tell him a Mr. Fargo is here?"

"We got a list, mister. The people who get in to see Mr. Tillman every day. And you ain't on that list."

"You sure about that?"

"Positive. Now you get outta here."

So Fargo did the only thing he could. Turned his stallion around and rode slowly away. A long, glum ride back to town. At least that's what he wanted them to think.

By the time Fargo had found a place to sneak on to the ranch, a half-moon hung in the sky like a tilted gold tear-drop. There were enough stars to give you a jolt, a sense of the whole vast universe that nobody could comprehend.

Fargo hid behind a copse of cottonwoods for two passes of the sentry. He timed them out. He would have approximately ten minutes to get on to the property and into the house.

The dog was also a problem, a handsome German shepherd that also walked the rough mile-long tract of this particular sentry section. The dog would be more of a threat because of its bark. Even if he eluded the handsome creature, the dog would alert both the sentry and the people in the house. Another sentry, maybe two, would join the dog.

He could shoot the dog but that, too, would attract attention. What he had to do was distract the dog's attention.

He ground-hitched his stallion and walked a quarter-mile to a wood as dark, yet moon-splashed, as any in a midnight ghost story. He spent only minutes before luckily finding a dying deer. He never killed needlessly. This animal was diseased, crying deep in its long, elegant throat, eyes rimed shut with crust.

He took out his knife and attempted to end its life quickly and painlessly. The elderly deer spasmed, made a faint noise, trembled for only a few seconds, and then sank into death. He slung it over his shoulder and walked back to his place in the cottonwoods.

He waited for the sentry to pass by again. He ran up an eighth of a mile with the deer, ducked beneath the barbed wire and pushed the body into plain sight.

He quickly vanished back into the shadows and ran back to the cottonwoods.

The dog picked up the scent almost immediately, running toward it with curiosity and clear joy.

Fargo dove for the barbed wire, belly-crawled beneath the fence, and jumped to his feet once he'd cleared the way.

He didn't even pause to see what the dog was doing. No time. He broke into a sprint that within a few minutes brought him to the grand mansion itself. The place resembled one of the English manor houses you always saw in pictures of the British countryside where the gentry lazed away their days fox hunting and having sex with the maids.

He knelt behind a large well. A guard with a shotgun stood in front of the side entrance, silhouetted against lamplight from inside.

One more obstacle to remove before he got inside and confronted Noah Tillman.

He fell back, rooting around on the shadowy earth until he found a rock of sufficient weight. Fargo had played in his share of throwing games, even pitched a little baseball in his time—strictly amateur stuff but a hell of a lot of fun—and he hoped his arm was up to the task tonight. There was no other way he could take the guard out. Rushing him would cost Fargo his life. And trying to sneak up on him would probably mean the same thing.

There was a large cottonwood just to the east of the side entrance, one that overlooked two picnic tables. It would be a long throw but this was the only cover he could find. As with the German shepherd, he'd have only one chance.

He hoped he knew what the hell he was doing.

On the ride back from what he hoped would be his last appointment of the day, Sheriff Tom Tillman thought about how tired he got of doing his stepfather's bidding.

It was now a few minutes after seven and he was just now getting back to his office from an incident he'd been forced to oversee. He wouldn't have dared sent a deputy because the incident had involved one of the local grandees who, if Noah had not shown up, would have complained to old Noah about how Tom should have handled this himself.

And then old Noah would rag on Tom's ass for an hour or two. Noah was just like Tom. He believed in strict control of his life. No surprises. The thing was, Noah had all of the money and most of the power and so when it came to a showdown between the two, Noah always won.

Tonight's incident had involved the grandee's drunken son holding a knife to his wife. The grandee didn't want anybody else to know about this, so he'd summoned Tom out there and Tom spent three hours trying to talk reason to the son. He insisted that his wife had been unfaithful. She insisted that the son was the unfaithful one. The problem was that the son had a butcher knife big enough to carve up a jungle elephant and was holding it to the slender, white throat of his fetching young wife, about whom Tom had had many fanciful fantasies himself.

Finally, Tom threw a bottle of expensive bourbon against the east wall of the bedroom they were all in. This distracted the drunken son just enough for Tom to jump him, wrench his wrist so hard he had to drop the knife, and then knock the stupid bastard unconscious with a single and impressive punch.

The young wife fell not into the arms of the grandee but

into the arms of the lawman. The way she moved against him ignited his loins and made him think that maybe his fantasies about her may someday come true.

The grandee was all gratitude and praise. And Tom was fittingly modest.

But as he rode back to town—he always checked in at the office before going home for the evening—the fantasy of the fetching wife began to fade, he started thinking about the man Fargo. The man seemed honest and, unless he was the killer, didn't have any reason to lie about the dead girl or her supposedly missing brother.

He'd never really discussed this with the old man. The travelers who turned up "missing" over the years. What was done with them. Why old Noah wanted them in the first place. Even if he'd asked, the old man wouldn't have told him. To Noah, Tom was both stepson and employee. And most of the time he treated Tom more like employee than son. Noah's brother Aaron—a drunken wastrel, according to most folks, but the best friend Tom had at the ranch—seemed to know something about these missing people, but would shut up when Noah scowled at him.

The way Noah seemed to feel was that he'd set Tom up as sheriff, built a nice house for him in town, made sure he married into a respectable family, and then urged Tom to begin having a brood of kids that stretched from here to sundown. Aaron often came to Tom's house to see the kids. He got along well with Tom's wife, too.

That was what he needed to do now. Get Uncle Aaron, as Tom had always called him, alone somewhere so they could talk without the threat of Noah walking in on them.

What the hell was going on here, anyway?

12

Maybe when his wandering days were over, Skye Fargo could get himself a job as a baseball pitcher.

The rock he threw at the burly man guarding the side entrance to Noah Tillman's mansion struck him right on the side of the head and pitched him sideways to the ground.

Fargo moved fast.

He jumped down on the man, striking him hard twice more on the side of the head to keep him out for awhile. He untied the man's bandana and used it to gag him with. He bound the man, wrists and ankles, with the man's belt and shirt. Fargo had learned long ago how to roll up a shirt so that it held like a strong, tight rope.

He eased up to the side door, put his ear to it, and crept inside.

He stood at the base of four stairs that led to a closed door. He drew his Colt, proceeded forward. Voices, now. Male. He listened again. The voices spoke in a Mexican dialect. He could piece together enough of the conversation to know that the voices belonged to servants. Apparently, they were finishing up their work for the day.

Fargo just hoped that neither one of them opened the door.

They finally broke up and went in separate directions. Fargo listened until their footsteps could no longer be heard.

The door. He stood on the second step, turned the doorknob, peered at what lay on the other side.

With the guttering sconces, the huge paintings, the pedestals bearing objets d'art of every kind, the marble floors, the vast hallway resembled a museum more than a home. Doors opened off of the hallway. He needed to get started. Somebody was likely to find that sentry soon enough.

He moved on tiptoe down the shadowy hall, the barrel of his Colt leading the way. The open doorways were easy to peer inside. The closed doors presented more of a danger. He listened first and then pushed his way through, but found no one. Each room was decorated so lavishly that the fussiness began to detract from what could have been a simple beauty. He suspected that all this represented not the taste of a tough old bastard like Noah Tillman but the taste of a woman decorator that Noah Tillman had hired. She must've been damned pretty to convince a ruthless land baron like Tillman to accept all this.

He spent fifteen minutes downstairs. The silence surprised him. The feeling was of a church late in the day, when nobody but old women prayed at the Communion rail.

He was just about to go upstairs—something he wasn't happy about, it being so damned easy to get trapped on a second floor—when he heard a male gringo voice barking an order. An order for a bourbon and water and *go easy on the water this time, dammit, Manuel.*

Noah Tillman, undoubtedly.

He'd been so intent on listening to Noah Tillman that he heard—too late—the faint shuffle of shoe leather behind him.

The cold reality of gun metal chilled the back of his neck.

"I do not believe you were invited here tonight," a Spanish voice said. "Now I will have to turn you over to the guards."

The man moved around in front of him. Fargo looked at the man who'd been shooting at him from the roof earlier today.

"He was your cousin?" Liz Turner asked.

"Yes, ma'am. My first cousin."

Her name was Bernice Cooper. She lived in a flat above an ice cream shop. She was old enough that her skin had a papery quality and her voice quavered from time to time. But her brown eyes gleamed with health and life. Liz had found her name among her late husband's notes on Noah Tillman, and decided to visit her. Apparently, Richard had never gotten around to it.

"And he came here why?"

"He worked on boats."

"Worked on?"

"Repaired them."

"I see."

A breeze came through the west window. In the lamplight, the small living room had a quaintness about it that made Liz feel at home. There was a couch, two chairs, a bookcase, and a tiny table where, she suspected, Bernice took each meal. The walls were covered with religious paintings.

"And he came here—"

"He came here to fix Noah Tillman's boat."

"There wasn't anybody who could do that locally?"

Bernice shrugged. "Bobby Lee was the best, I guess. At least that's what folks said. Plus he wasn't that far away. Just a day's ride, over to Simpson."

"And you saw him?"

Bernice nodded. "Two or three times. He took me out for supper twice. He was a nice man, Bobby Lee."

"You think he's dead?"

"I don't know what else I *could* think. He just vanished. Never came around to see me again, never went back to his own place, either. He was just—gone."

"Did you ever talk to Noah Tillman about him?"

She made a face. "You ever try to talk to Noah Tillman about anything? He just sort of waves you away, like he'd never stoop low enough to speak to you."

"And all this was—"

"Two years ago. About now, in fact. Fourth of July coming up and everything."

Liz was trying to make some sense of this story. The woman wasn't a hysteric, wasn't accusing anybody of anything, hadn't even asked for help. Liz had had to seek Bernice out. But here was one more tale of "vanishing," one that Richard had found during the course of his investigation, one that he'd obviously planned to follow up. She now planned to talk to every person Richard had listed in his notes about this story.

"If I could ever get a grand jury together, would you be willing to testify to all this?" Liz said.

"Why, sure."

"A lot of people are afraid of Noah Tillman."

Bernice laughed. "Well, I'm not one of them, Missy. The way he treated me when I asked him about Bobby Lee— well, to hell with him. Excuse my language."

Liz stood up. "I appreciate all the help you've been, Bernice."

Bernice walked her to the door. "It's the least I could do for Bobby Lee. He was a good man."

Noah Tillman had an outsize head and white ringlets that together resembled the bust of a Roman senator or general.

He sat all splendid in his chair in his splendid study and when the servant brought Fargo in at gunpoint, he looked up with a splendid smile and said, "Thank you, Manuel. I was looking for a little entertainment this evening."

Fargo hadn't known what to expect. He still didn't. Noah Tillman was treating this situation as if the carnival had just rolled into town.

Manuel explained, in Spanish, that he'd found Fargo lurking in the grand hall and brought him directly to the study.

"But, Manuel, you don't seem to realize that our guest has a considerable reputation." Noah Tillman's droll tone continued. "He's known as the Trailsman. And he seems to've earned his reputation. He's a fast man with a gun. And a smart one, too, I'm told. Are you smart, Mr. Fargo?"

"Apparently not," Fargo said, matching Noah Tillman's tone. "Manuel here caught me, didn't he?"

The way Noah Tillman's head was angled to the right reminded Fargo that the man was hard of hearing.

"Yes, but in order to get into the house, you had to get through a dog and a sentry and another guard."

Fargo smiled. "Well, maybe I *am* smart, after all."

"Manuel, get us a drink. How does a brandy sound, Mr. Fargo? And please, take a chair."

Now what the hell was this all about? Fargo wondered. You catch a man invading your property and your house and you invite him to have a drink?

Well, whatever was going on here—and something

clearly was—Fargo didn't have much choice but to sit down and find out what it was.

Tom Tillman was just leaving the sheriff's office when he realized that he wouldn't be able to keep his pledge after all. He had promised himself that he would avoid seeing Liz Turner until he could get control of his feelings again. Though he didn't love his wife, he respected her and respected the vows he'd taken when they'd gotten married, even though his father had bullied him into the union. Sara came from a "prestigious" family. And Noah, for all his rough ways, liked the idea of being prestigious. And then Tom got Sara pregnant and there had been no choice. As soon as she was confirmed with child, the marriage was hastily put together.

But for the first time in his life, he was in love. And it was a guilty, painful thing that haunted and taunted his days as well as his nights. But he couldn't give Liz up. Couldn't and wouldn't.

He stood on the raised sidewalk and when she reached him, he helped her up.

She waved a note at him. "Your father is going to have company tonight, Tom."

"Oh?"

"Fargo is planning on paying him a visit." She paused and said, "I'm sorry about the other night, Tom."

"It was my fault."

She laughed. He loved that rich, womanly laugh of hers. "Well, let's share the guilt, then."

"It won't happen again." He'd gotten angry at himself that night, said that he had no business being with her, made her, as she'd said through her tears, "feel like a whore."

She touched his arm. He felt a passion he tried to deny. There in the moonlight, he saw the face of the woman he loved. Not just for sex, or because she seemed to understand him. But because she'd done all the things he'd wanted to do—gone off on her own and faced the world and wrestled it to the ground. Her terrible childhood in the streets of Baltimore where she survived by being a thief in her early teen years. And then working in a convent as a trade-off with the nuns who taught her to read and write, until she ventured west to get into the raw and often dangerous business of frontier journalism.

There was warmth and wisdom in this woman. No bitterness. No remorse. And seemingly no fear. He ached for her sexually but he ached for her in so many other ways, too.

"Something's going on here, Tom. Fargo knows it and I know it. And you know it, too, but out of loyalty to Noah, you won't look into it. I don't like the idea of Fargo going out to the mansion. Too many people have vanished in the last ten years." She hesitated. "I had to say that, Tom."

"I know. I've been thinking about it myself."

"Would you be willing to confront Noah about it?"

"I guess I don't have much choice, do I?" He paused. "I need to get home. I haven't been spending enough time with the kids."

That was another thing he admired about Liz. Where other women in her position would resent the time he spent with his family, she encouraged it. She'd come from such bitter circumstances herself that she didn't want his children to endure the same pain.

"We'll talk tomorrow," she said.

She was soon lost in the night as she made her way back to the newspaper office.

"You've made quite a name for yourself, Mr. Fargo," Noah Tillman said.

Cigars, brandy, a crackling fireplace, deep leather chairs. And a courteous host who should, by rights, be mad as hell because Fargo had trespassed on his property.

"I'm sort of curious, Mr. Tillman."

"Noah is fine."

"All right, Noah it is. Why aren't you having me arrested?"

Tillman made a sweeping, dramatic gesture with his cigar-filled hand. "Because I believe somebody is using you to get to me. And I want to set you straight. I don't want you to think ill of my little town. And it is 'my' town, Mr. Fargo, as everybody will tell you."

"Set me straight about what? About why Manuel shot at me this afternoon?"

Noah smiled. "Manuel gets very protective of me. Sometimes, he gets carried away."

Sip of brandy. Long pull on his cigar. Exhaling the smoke through the side of his mouth, his outsize cuff link catching the golden light of the desk lamp. "I want to set you straight about this legend people like to keep alive. This legend about vanishing people, Mr. Fargo."

"Then it's not true?"

Noah laughed. "It's true if you're the type who believes in vampires and werewolves. You hear those kinds of stories, too. And not just from Indians. From a lot of white people in town. They're always seeing zombies and things like that. And for the past seven or eight years, they've convinced themselves that a number of visitors have disappeared." He smiled, his eyes considering the heft of his cigar. "I'm sure they think that werewolves carted them off."

"Whenever people in your town don't want to talk about the missing folks, they try to say it's all as crazy as werewolves and vampires. And anyway, if you don't have anything to do with it, why would you care what people think?"

"For a very simple reason, Mr. Fargo. This town, as I said, is mine. I built it, I support it, I'm getting it ready for the future. But what kind of a future are we going to have if there are all these stories about vanishing people going around? Would you want to settle in a town like that?"

Fargo sipped some of his brandy. Excellent. But then would you expect less from a man like Noah Tillman? "Has there ever been a serious investigation into these disappearances?"

"Several, by the man who was sheriff before my son."

"He was also a relative of yours, I believe," Fargo said.

"That doesn't discredit him."

"You said there were several investigations."

"That's right," Noah said, brushing some ash from his smoking jacket. "Including one by the local newspaperman."

"He was killed if I'm not mistaken," Fargo said. "Backshot, I believe."

"That's true. But it didn't have anything to do with the so-called disappearances."

"That isn't what the man's widow told me."

"Ah, Liz," Noah said grandly. "Quite a figure on that lady, isn't there?"

Fargo said nothing.

"And she's quite a newspaperwoman, too. Good editor, I mean. Knows what sells and what doesn't sell. Knows that if you want to keep your readers happy, you have to give them raw red meat. And what's the best way to do that? Why, attack powerful people. Your everyday, average person resents powerful people. And loves to hear hints that powerful people are untrustworthy and corrupt. You can't go wrong with stories like that and Liz knows it. So she's always coming after me. And with anything she can get her hands on. She still tells anybody who'll listen that I had her husband shot. And the same with how I run my various businesses. That I bribe legislators whenever I want to get a right-of-way or want to get some kind of edge on my competition. She's even implied in a couple of stories that I was behind several fires my competitors suffered."

"And you weren't?"

Noah paused and looked solemnly at Fargo. "Do you hear how I speak? I have a second grade education, Mr. Fargo. But when I got wealthy, I hired a tutor. I even learned a little about art and serious music. We have musicals out here sometimes. My late wife, God love her, wanted me to become a civilized man and by God I did it.

"And the same with business, Mr. Fargo. Everything I've got, I got for myself. Of course I've cut a few legal corners here and there—when all else fails, I'm perfectly willing to bribe a few state legislators, that's just part of the business—but I don't do anything that my competitors don't do. And I sure as hell don't spirit visitors away when they come to town. Think about it, Mr. Fargo. Why would I do something like that? What would I do with these people? And what would I get out of it?"

He was pretty damned convincing. He'd be tough in a court of law. He would overpower all but the most clever of prosecuting attorneys. And he'd do it all with reason, a rich and deep voice, and absolute charm.

"So there's nothing to it."

"If there was, do you think I'd invite you in to have a drink and explain myself? I'd have you arrested. Discredited. So that nobody would listen to what you have to say." He rose, ending the meeting. "I invited you because I have nothing to hide." The smile. "And because I knew that a man of your reputation would probably enjoy a rest and a little expensive brandy. You've had an awful lot of adventures in your life, Mr. Fargo."

Fargo finished his brandy, stood up, accepted the hand this splendid, domineering actor offered him. He hadn't believed a word of it—was convinced now that Noah Tillman did indeed have something to hide—but decided to pretend that he'd been taken in. "Appreciate the brandy." He picked up his hat.

The servant appeared in the doorway.

"Manuel will show you out, Mr. Fargo. I enjoyed meeting you."

Manuel walked him to the front door. His steps were loud, especially on the long stretch of parquet flooring.

"You're a pretty lousy shot, Manuel."

"I have nothing to say."

"But even lousy shots get lucky once in a while."

"Please. We should not be having this conversation."

"The thing is, I kind of resent being shot at. I'd guess that's a pretty normal reaction, wouldn't you? Man's walking down an alley to save some time and there's this shooter up on a roof trying to kill him."

They reached the door. Manuel opened it for him.

Fargo caught him just below the sternum. Manuel might be a slick, tricky protector of the old man's but he couldn't take a punch worth a damn. He bent in half, staggered out onto the porch, and promptly threw up.

"I'd say we're about even now," Fargo said as he prepared himself for the lengthy walk back to his horse.

Ten minutes later, Fargo was on his stallion and headed back to the main road when he saw another horse and rider leaving the estate and heading toward town. From a distance, traced by moonlight, the rider resembled Noah Tillman. White hair, wide shoulders, imposing stature.

But where would Noah Tillman be headed at this time and at this speed? Wasn't he the kind of man who did all his work through his hired gunnies?

Fargo reached the road and started toward town. The

rider was still behind him but closing fast. Fargo's Ovaro stallion loped along.

When the rider was still some distance back, Fargo's hand slid to his Colt. Since he didn't know what the hell was going on here, he wanted to be ready for whatever happened.

The rider did some talking to his horse. The timber of his voice was much like Noah Tillman's. The rider's horse slowed so that it could match the lope of Fargo's stallion.

"Evening, Mr. Fargo."

His first impression was that he was looking at Noah Tillman. Only after staring at the rider did he see the difference. The nose straighter. The eyes slightly larger. The subtle air of menace not present in the gaze nor the way the rider held himself. Otherwise, he could have been Noah himself with the expensive suit and the pure-bred horse.

"The name's Aaron. Noah's brother." A crooked and somewhat sad smile further set him apart from his sibling. "I'm sure you've heard of me. When the town isn't talking about what a ruthless bastard my brother is, they're talking about what a drunken, gambling, womanizer *I* am."

"Sounds like you're having a good time, anyway."

"I am, as a matter of fact. Except when my brother puts me in one of those special hospitals they have for the insane. He dries me out and I stay clean for a while and then go back to my old ways."

The sadness that had been in his smile was now in his voice. He'd made a pass at sounding like a merry drunkard and degenerate but you could tell he didn't have any more respect for himself than Noah did. Noah wouldn't be forgiving of weakness.

Fargo let him do the talking—or not talking. They rode in silence for some time, the hooves of their horses loud in the humid air and the half-moon world of this night.

"I was hoping to catch up with you, Mr. Fargo."

"Oh? And why would that be?"

Aaron had inherited the family penchant for drama. He let a long moment go by and then said, "I thought I'd tell you what happened to all those missing people."

73

13

Fifteen minutes after the Trailsman left, Noah Tillman heard a knock on his study door and said, "Enter."

Manuel came in the room briskly. He belonged to another era. He would have been home in medieval Europe when each castle required more than its share of spies and courtesans.

"Excuse me, sir."

"What is it, Manuel?" Noah sounded irritable and with good reason. He'd been looking over some construction bills that made him suspicious. He wondered if the man he'd put in charge of this particular job had made some kind of arrangement with the man building a new warehouse in the southern part of the state. The bill seemed twice as high as necessary. Hadn't his man gotten bids? It was so easy to lard construction contracts. The builder padded the bill and then gave a good percentage of the extra money to Noah's man. Noah would tend to this first thing in the morning.

"It's about your brother, sir."

Noah sighed and said wryly, "Bad news, of course, Manuel?"

"I assume so, sir."

"Been trying to get into my safe again?"

"No, sir."

"Stealing wine from my personal collection in the basement?"

"Afraid not, sir."

"Then it's really serious?"

"It could be, sir. That's why I thought you ought to know what's going on."

Noah pitched the invoices he'd been studying to his desk top, leaned back in in his chair, closed his eyes, and said, "What's he up to now, Manuel?"

"I watched him saddle up his horse about half an hour ago. But he didn't leave the ranch."

"No? Then what did he do?"

"He waited in the pines to the north of the house, sir."

"Any particular reason?"

"That's what I couldn't figure out, sir. But then Fargo left and your brother followed him."

With his eyes opened wide, Noah sat upright in his tall leather chair. "Followed him? For what?"

"I'm not sure why he'd follow him, sir. But right now they're on the stage road. Talking."

"You followed them?"

"Yessir. But I couldn't get close enough to hear what they were actually saying."

But Noah was already speculating on what they might be saying. What with all the sudden talk about the disappearances, he knew damned well what they might be saying. The time had finally come—as he knew it would someday—to deal with his brother in a permanent way. This wasn't about liquor or gambling or womanizing. This was about something far more basic. This was about trust. After all that Noah had done for Aaron.

"When he comes back here, I want him locked in his room."

"Yessir."

"Have Ekert help you. Wait up 'til Aaron comes home, do you understand?"

"Yessir."

"No matter what time it is."

"Yessir."

After Manuel left, Noah sat brooding in his chair, in his study, in his mansion, in the area of the state that could truly be called "his." He should have felt all-powerful and completely invulnerable. But vulnerability and betrayal creeped in. Aaron didn't know as much about Noah's "special project" as he probably thought he did. But he knew just enough to point a man like Fargo in the right direction. And Fargo, with this new information was going to be a problem for sure.

He got up, poured himself more brandy, and carried the snifter to one of the long, mullioned windows. He'd always known that he would someday have to murder his brother, that Aaron would force him to commit the ultimate crime. The time was here and now.

This did not make him happy. But what could he do? Aaron could bring it all down, everything, unless he was stopped and stopped for good.

Noah wondered for a long time if he could actually do it. His own brother? He stared out at the starry night. But what was he thinking? Of course he could do it. What other choice did he have?

"It's called Skeleton Key," Aaron Tillman said. "It's an island about ten miles from the bluffs you see on the east end of our property. A man named Deke Burgade operates it for my brother. Supposedly, he's checking out the minerals there. But it's been going on for five years. The island's big but not that big. And Burgade is no mineral expert. He's a tough who's worked for Noah for at least ten years."

They sat their horses just off the road. The warm night lacquered both of them with sweat. The moonlight gave an ominous yet beautiful look to the countryside.

"I'm not sure what all this has to do with these disappearances," Fargo said.

"I'm not, either, exactly. But since the disappearances have taken place around the Fourth of July every year, and since Burgade always shows up at about the same time—in the house, I mean; he rarely leaves the island—I'm just wondering if there isn't some connection."

Fargo watched the man. Aaron seemed sober but not comfortably so. His arms and his voice shook. And he kept licking his dry lips.

"I guess I'm wondering why'd you go against your brother this way?"

"Because I know what my brother's like. He's had some strange—pastimes, I guess you'd call them."

"Like what?"

"Well, there was a time when he led every posse that had to be got up."

"A lot of men join posses."

"Not posses like these. He'd take only trackers. He

wouldn't let them use their firearms unless it was self-defense. He wanted them to locate the fugitive and then come and get him. He insisted on killing the fugitive himself."

"He never brought them in alive?"

"Never." Aaron took out a long, thin cigar, bit off the end, spat it out. The lucifer was bright in the bird-cry darkness. He inhaled smoke deeply and then exhaled it. "He always worked it around so that he had some excuse to kill the man. And nobody was about to challenge him. You don't challenge my brother. Or maybe you've learned that already."

Another long drag on the cigar. "And that isn't all, Fargo. A couple of prostitutes visited his fishing cabin over the years and were never seen or heard from again."

"No explanation?"

"None. Nobody really gives a damn when soiled doves vanish anyway. And also you come back to the same problem—who's going to challenge Noah?"

"I hear his stepson is pretty honest."

"Very honest. And a good lawman. But I convinced him to let the whole thing slide."

"Hell," Fargo said, "why would you do that?"

"Simple. I like the boy. Even with all my personal problems, I've always been more of a father to him than Noah ever was. I don't want to see him get himself killed."

"Your brother would kill his own stepson?"

"If he felt he needed to."

The Trailsman had met many different kinds of people during his years of wandering through this noisy, vibrant country called America but he'd met only a very few who'd turn on their own blood kin. Aaron and Noah Tillman had to genuinely despise each other for Aaron to give him this kind of information. Or was Aaron simply using him? What if he was lying about Noah so that Fargo would go after him? It wouldn't be the first time a weak man had tricked a surrogate into doing his work for him.

But Aaron was convincing enough that Fargo knew he'd have to investigate these allegations. People were disappearing and so far this was the first reasonable explanation he'd heard.

"Aren't you afraid of your brother?" Fargo asked.

77

"Terrified of him."

"Then why don't you leave?"

Aaron sighed. "Because life is too easy for me here. I get drunk and he dries me out. And in the meantime, I get to live in a mansion, eat the best food available, and have servants wait on me hand and foot. I'm not exactly an honorable man, Mr. Fargo. I leech off my brother because it's the only way I can keep myself in a steady supply of liquor. My visits to the hospitals are short enough. And then I come right back and start imbibing again. Free of charge. I drink only the best brands of liquor, too. And Noah pays for it."

He paused. "But I can't countenance murder—or whatever the hell's going on with my brother. I need to find out what Noah has been up to all these years. And you can help me."

Fargo nodded. "I'll see what I can do, Aaron." He gripped the reins tighter on his stallion and said, "You might think of moving out. Might do you some good to stand on your own two feet."

Aaron said, "You sound like a preacher, Mr. Fargo."

Fargo laughed. "Now that's the one thing nobody's ever accused me of before."

He set off for town, his stallion loping along the moonlit road.

Aaron wasn't sure why but the mansion seemed unnaturally quiet to him when he returned. If nothing else, the servants usually made noise as they prepared the house for bedtime. But not now.

He was headed up the vast, sweeping staircase when Manuel stepped from the shadows and said, "Mr. Tillman would like to see you, sir."

Aaron, sensing the danger of the moment—something in the shadowed peek he'd gotten at Manuel's face ahead alarmed him—tried to appear at ease. "You know, Manuel, my name is Mr. Tillman, too. That could get confusing sometimes."

There were pets that belonged strictly to one member of the family. As a child, he'd spent so much time with a kitten named Buttons that the animal didn't want to play with anybody but Aaron. It was like that with Manuel. He answered only to Noah. He had no other boss. The most anybody else got from him was cold obedience. But you could tell that he could barely tolerate you—unless you were the one and only Noah.

"Is he in the study?"

"Yes, sir."

"Thank you."

There had been times when he was drunk that he'd gotten abusive with Manuel. But not when he was sober. When he was sober, he treated Manuel as if he were the boss and Aaron the servant. Couldn't help it. Manuel's imperious manner always intimidated him.

Manuel slipped away, leaving Aaron to consider how to prepare himself for what he knew would be a confrontation with his brother. Had Noah discovered the three bottles of whiskey he had stolen from the basement? Had Noah received all the bills from his last binge at the whorehouse, when he'd sat naked with three whores and given them two thousand dollars to divide—two thousand dollars he'd had to borrow from the madame? You never knew what would piss Noah off. Sometimes he'd let some pretty outrageous things slide. Other times he'd jump all over him for practically nothing.

Aaron considered running away. He'd always known that some day Noah would no longer tolerate him. Would deal him with a very un-brotherly severity. Had Noah reached that point? Had Noah changed from his reluctant protector into his disgusted enemy? To run away . . . but where? And with what money? He'd be back begging at Noah's door in no time. Always the same for Aaron—the boy-man who'd never grown up. The boy-man who'd always live at the mercy of his brother.

What did Noah want tonight?

Well, there was only one way to find out.

He walked down the stairs on legs that were now shaking. Patting his hair into place. Daubing at his sweaty face with a handkerchief. His stomach was sour, mean. Damn Noah anyway. Just once Aaron would like to put his brother through this kind of drill and see how *he* liked it.

Noah was standing in the center of his study when Aaron crossed the threshold. His smile was almost a smirk. "You're a very sociable fellow, brother."

"What's that supposed to mean?"

"I'm told you followed Mr. Fargo when he left here."

"That damned Manuel. Why can't he mind his own business?"

"He's minding *my* business. He thought I might be interested in why you followed Fargo."

"I wanted to invite him to a party I'm having in town tomorrow night. On the Fourth of July."

"He accepted your invitation, of course."

"He said he'd think it over."

Noah didn't speak for a time. He just stood there looking at his brother. Aaron was surprised to find an expression of real hurt on his brother's face. "I've taken care of you all of my life, brother. Every single day. I've bought you out of jail, I've paid off your gambling debts, I tried to wean you off the bottle by paying exorbitant rates at those hospitals you went to. And you've never shown me the slightest gratitude. Never a thank you. Never an offer to help me when I was having problems. Never even a friendly word."

"I didn't realize you were such a sensitive flower," Aaron said, and instantly knew that he'd picked the wrong time for sarcasm.

Noah's face tightened. The expression of hurt feelings shifted now into the more familiar one of cold contempt. "Luckily for me, I don't give a damn anymore, Aaron. I don't feel any obligation to protect you—especially since you're doing everything you can to get me into trouble."

"Meaning what?"

"Meaning that you know damned well what Fargo was doing here. He wanted to know about the people who've gone missing around here. You're just like my stepson. You'd both be happy to bring me down. And you see Fargo as the man to do it."

There was a five-step difference separating the two men. Noah crossed it in swift, purposeful steps. Then, without feinting, without warning, he drove his fist so hard into Aaron's stomach that the man was driven to his knees.

"Now, brother," Noah said, "you're going to tell me everything you've been able to figure out about my little island. I want to know exactly what Fargo knows."

14

By the time he reached town, Fargo saw that some of the revelers had already taken to the main street. American flags, bunting, and banners festooned the street. A band consisting of an accordion, trombone, and fiddle played some pretty terrible dance music while drunks of both sexes careened and caromed through big, dramatic steps that looked more like wrestling than dancing.

Light was provided by a small bonfire overseen by a night deputy and his shotgun. You could have fun but not *too* much fun. Firelight played on the glazed, sweaty faces of the imbibers, giving their features mask-like qualities.

Just after dawn, this street would be jammed with wagons, buckboards, buggies, and men, women, and children of every kind. The state had entered the Union in 1836 and was proud of it.

Fargo went straight to his hotel. In the morning, he'd contact Liz Turner and share with her what he'd learned from Aaron.

He was one step into his room when a young, seductive female voice said, "No need to turn the lamp up, Mr. Fargo. I'm still on duty so this will have to be fast, I'm afraid."

Now, how could you turn that down?

Even as he was dropping his trousers, she leaned forward and guided him to the bed with his rigid shaft, which she promptly began to stroke as if it were holy.

When he got on the bed and straddled her, she began to rub his massive tool against her breasts, her nipples coming erect instantly as her hips began to writhe and her throat fill with moans.

Only when her entire body was wracked with desire did she move his unbending rod down to the dark beauty between her legs. Once again, she teased both of them by running the tip of him up and down the lips of her sex. He began to moan as much as she did, sliding his huge arms under her small body and easing himself into her.

She'd wanted it fast and she got it fast, the two of them caught up as one in the play of their bodies. He surprised her by moving them both to the edge of the bed where she sat on his lap and began to bounce up and down on his shaft, biting his shoulder hard to suppress that animal scream yearning for freedom. But such a scream would only get her in trouble. Somebody might report her to the manager.

Fargo wanted to do his own screaming when he poured himself into her, her relentless grinding of his shaft causing him to have a moment that felt a little bit like dying— everything stopped—there was only the searing pleasure of their lust and the exquisite tautness of her buttocks in his hands.

As she was shuddering and falling into him, he blessed her nipples with a quick kiss, and she shuddered all the more.

Fargo had to give them credit. They'd worked out a pretty effective plan.

He woke to the sound of the revelers, wondering what time it was. The drinkers and the dancers were going to be completely spent by dawn. They'd spend the Fourth tending to hangovers instead of getting into the fun.

Darkness. The faint squeak of a doorknob in need of oil as it was turned to the right. Fargo slid his hand to the floor, where he kept his Colt. He filled his hand with it as he came up off the bed, waiting for his intruder.

A silhouette of a man in the tallest western hat Fargo had ever seen. Too bad the man wasn't as slick at his hat. He came creeping in on cowboy boots with all the grace of an elephant turned ballerina. Always in sight thanks to the flickering sconce in the hall.

The intruder's eyes obviously hadn't adjusted to the darkness yet.

Fargo said, "Hand the gun over, mister."

Fargo stepped out of the gloom and slapped the barrel of his Colt across the face of the startled, blinking man.

Since he resented being wakened from a sound sleep, Fargo swatted the man around for a time, hitting him on the jaw, knocking the wind out of him with a punch delivered straight to his sternum. He finished by taking the man's fancy new six-shooter from him.

He was just busy enough that his mind didn't quite register the other sound in the room. By the time he started to turn, it was too late.

A man was climbing through the window where there was a fire escape that ran from ground to roof. The man had had no problem.

"Couple of ways we can do this, Fargo. Your way or my way." He pointed a sawed-off, double-barreled shotgun at Fargo. "Toss your gun onto the bed."

Fargo recognized the voice of the white man who'd been with the Mexican yesterday morning. They'd taken Daisy.

The gunny who had come through the door was picking himself up and cursing. He'd just been humiliated and physically hurt in the process.

He staggered to the table and turned up the lamp.

"Name's Ekert," said the man with the shotgun. "Guess I didn't have a chance to introduce myself yesterday."

"Let's get going," said his partner. He was still nervous from the humiliation. A man like him preferred to think of himself as tough. That was the only thing he could claim to be. Smart, no. Cunning, no. Successful, no. But tough—damned tough. Except he wasn't damned tough, was he? Not anymore, not in the eyes of Ekert, anyway.

"We're taking a trip, Mr. Fargo." Ekert glanced around the room suspiciously, as if expecting a leprechaun with a six-gun to be hiding somewhere.

"Same kind of trip you took Daisy on?"

"Believe it or not, nobody told the Mex to kill her," Ekert said. "He was just supposed to keep her hidden 'till the boat came."

The boat. Fargo thought about the island Aaron Tillman had alluded to. Maybe this was the fastest way to find out what was going on. Let himself become a captive of these two gunnies—given the fact that they had the drop on him didn't leave him much choice, anyway—and see if that led him to the boat and the island.

"Get your clothes on," Ekert said.

"You're gonna be sorry you hit me," said the other gunny.

Fargo dressed.

"I take it Noah sent you," he said as he pulled on his boots.

"Who sent us is none of your business," Ekert said.

"It's gonna be a pleasure to pay you back," the other gunny said.

"We don't hurt him," Ekert said. "The island, remember?"

"The Mexican was a lot tougher than this one," Fargo said, smiling at the other gunny. "This one isn't tough and he isn't smart."

Fargo saw an easy chance for escape. He could smash the lamp. He was close enough to the open window to dive through. In the darkness, Ekert wouldn't be able to figure out what was going on until it was too late.

But as salty—not to mention crazy—Cap'n Bill had told him, the easiest way to get on the island was to have somebody kidnap him and take him there.

Well, here was his chance.

He buttoned his shirt, hefted his manhood to a more comfortable angle inside his breeches, and then said, "Let's go, gentlemen."

"What the hell're you so happy about?" the other gunny asked.

"Well, hell, friend," Fargo said. "It's the Fourth of July. Why wouldn't I be happy?"

"He sounds like he's got somethin' funny planned," the other gunny said to Ekert.

"Shut up," Ekert said.

They left the room by way of the fire escape.

15

Fargo was thrown into the back of a buckboard, marked by slivers in the wood of the wagon bed. He lay beneath a horse blanket that smelled of animal urine and hay. Ekert and the other gunny sat up front.

It was hot as hell, and his sweat added to the urine scent and the bouncing ride to make the trip miserable. Plus it made him need to piss. But he'd play hell getting them to stop and let him empty his bladder.

He was hoping they'd talk to each other, fill in a few details about where they were going and what their plans were. But they said nothing.

Fargo stared into the darkness.

Somehow, despite everything working against it, Fargo managed to drift into a light sleep.

He woke to find that the buckboard had pulled off to the side of the stage road.

"Where are we?" he said.

"Don't worry about it, Fargo," Ekert said.

"Yeah, don't worry about it, Fargo," the other gunny said, sounding like a dumb little kid imitating his old man.

The silence returned.

After awhile the other gunny said, "They're late."

"Yeah, I noticed that, McGarth," Ekert said sarcastically. "I'm sittin' here with you, remember?"

"Who they bringin' us?"

"I don't know. All Manuel said was that we were to meet 'em here and they'd have somebody else for the boat."

"Well, they're late," McGarth said.

Ekert sighed. "You say that one more time, McGarth, and I'm makin' you walk."

The silence again. Fargo had a few second thoughts about putting his fate in the hands of two idiots like these. What was to say McGarth wouldn't say "screw it" and shoot him, anyway? Fargo had humiliated him, or that was how McGarth saw it, and it was obvious the man was eager to pay Fargo back.

After a long time, the clatter of an approaching wagon could be heard.

"About time," McGarth said.

Fargo tried to sit up but the way they had lashed his wrists and ankles made it impossible to raise his head more than a few inches. But at least when he sat up this way, the blanket fell away and the air, hot as it was, smelled clean.

The buckboard pulled up alongside the wagon.

"How come you're so late, Manuel?" McGarth said, sounding angry.

"I don't answer to you," Manuel sneered.

"Never mind him, Manuel. I thought maybe something went wrong."

"Something *did* go wrong. My friend here managed to escape when we were loading him on the buckboard. He faked being unconscious. You'll have to watch him carefully. He's a wily one."

"He ain't gonna escape while I'm around," McGarth said.

Manuel laughed. "You have a brave one with you, I see, Mr. Ekert."

"If he was as good with his gun as he is with his mouth, he'd be a dangerous man," Ekert laughed.

"You two think you're pretty funny, don't you?"

"Go help him load up the other one," Ekert said to McGarth.

In the moon shadow night, a second man bound identically to Fargo was carried from Manuel's buckboard to the wagon holding Fargo. He was loaded next to Fargo with all the tender care of two-by-fours being crammed into a wagon bed.

"We meet again, Mr. Fargo."

The voice surprised Fargo. He rolled slightly so he could get a look at the man who'd just spoken in such familiar tones.

Aaron Tillman.

"I guess tonight we'll both find out what the island is all about," Aaron said. "The big secret, I mean."

"Shut up back there," McGarth said.

"Right now all I care about," Fargo said, loudly enough to be heard by all, "is to give McGarth a nice big funeral."

Manuel, obviously trusting neither Ekert nor McGarth, came back to the wagon bed and jumped up to check the ropes that lashed the men. This was something Ekert and McGarth should have thought of but had forgotten.

"You'll have fun on the island," Manuel said, still wearing the uniform-like clothes from earlier this evening. "It's a real adventure—for everybody involved."

"You're not going to give us a hint about it?" Fargo said.

"I would not want to spoil your pleasure in discovering for yourself, Mr. Fargo."

"That's very thoughtful of you, Manuel."

"But I will say this. You'll never see the games on the island played anywhere else. Nobody would have the courage Mr. Tillman does."

"You sure you're not confusing courage with insanity, Manuel?" Aaron said.

"I hate to say this to you, Mr. Aaron, but I think you're jealous of your brother. You resent the fact that he's so—creative. The only thing you're creative with is finishing off a fifth of whiskey before anybody else. I have to give you that. You have an enormous capacity. For that I salute you."

"We're going to die, aren't we?" Aaron said.

Manuel laughed softly. "As I said, I don't want to spoil your pleasure and fun. You need to discover the island all for yourself."

He jumped down from the bed and walked around front.

"Straight to the dock, Ekert."

"I know, Manuel."

"Mr. Tillman will be on the island later this morning. He'll expect them to be there. But you're not to wait. You're to come back as soon as these two are delivered."

Ekert sighed again. Another deep, frustrated sigh. "I know my orders, Manuel. I'm not stupid, you know."

"I just want you to know the consequences if something should go wrong. These are the people Mr. Tillman wants."

"And he'll have them. Now stand aside. I want to get going."

The buckboard began to roll again. The second half of the journey was no more or no less hot and uncomfortable than the first half.

Aaron talked a good deal of the time, sharing more stories about his brother's strange habits. "He got so jaded that he had to start upping the ante. Instead of one whore in his bed, he had to have two, then three. And the sex acts got a lot more sadistic. He's pretty much barred from all the best houses in Little Rock. None of the whores'll go with him. They're too afraid."

On and on into the night this way, each new tale more outrageous than the last. Finally, Fargo was lucky enough to drift off to sleep again.

Tom Tillman woke early, kissed his sleeping wife and children, and headed, without even the mercy of a cup of coffee, to the office.

The town was quiet and solemn and lovely in the breaking dawn. There was a slight haze over everything, blunting some of the ferocious coloring of the Fourth of July decorations. A couple of men were passed out in chairs on the porch of a saloon; another man slept in a buggy without a horse attached. Here and there you could see articles of female attire in the dust or hanging from the end of a hitching post or lying over a porch railing.

Wait 'til tomorrow morning, he thought. The aftermath of a Fourth of July spectacle always left the town looking like a battlefield. This was the only time of year when even most of the churchgoers let themselves go. And the visitors let themselves go even further.

The night deputy sat at his desk filling out forms. When he looked up and saw Tillman, he said, "Believe it or not, Sheriff, we've got a full house. They finally settled down and went to sleep."

"Anything serious?"

"Busted nose, broken arm, couple black eyes, and soon there'll be a whole lot of bad hangovers. But nobody was shot, stabbed, or set on fire so I figure it was a pretty good night."

Tillman would usually smile at such a rueful assessment.

But he was too tensed up with his mission to have any fun. "I'll be in my office."

"Yessir."

Tillman poured himself some coffee and headed to the hall. No lamplight was needed. The sun was starting to clear through the haze. The office window was painted a frail golden color.

He set his cup of coffee on top of the second filing cabinet and went to work. He'd hired a widow who'd been desperately in need of money to set his files in strict order. She'd done so good a job that using the files now intimidated him. Afraid he'd screw up the system she'd established, he was extra careful to put each file back as soon as he was finished with it.

He spent an hour working on the names and dates of the reports on missing people from town. Most of them had no relevance to the "vanished" people that Fargo had asked him about. But between Liz's husband being shot because he was investigating the situation and Fargo identifying one of the men who'd burst into his room as Ekert, he knew that his stepfather was involved in this. And he also knew that the stories were true. People did vanish around here this time every year. And if his stepfather's men were involved in "disappearing" Daisy this year, it was likely they'd been involved in the other years as well.

The boat. The island.

What the hell was Noah up to anyway?

He prepared the paperwork the way a lawyer would prepare a trial. He wanted not to merely confront Noah but to assault him with names and dates. See how the cold, old bastard reacted when faced with so many incidents of people just disappearing.

He thought again of his mother and wondered, as he'd wondered ever since he'd come to stay with the Tillmans, what had ever drawn her to Noah. A simple, good woman drawn to a devious, morally corrupt bully like Noah Tillman made no sense to Tom.

He snorted a laugh. Hell, Noah might not even let him on his property this morning. Noah was still angry that Tom had refused to arrest a farmer, a small part of whose land Noah wanted to the east of his property. It was Noah's intention to build a fancy horse-breeding business there.

He could easily have built it somewhere else but once Noah got something into his head, he pursued it ruthlessly. The farmer didn't want to sell. He wasn't being ornery. He liked a hill that particular stretch of land had at its western end. He and his family had picnics there in the summer and in winter his kids used it for sledding and sliding. It was nothing against Noah, the farmer insisted. He just liked that piece of land and wanted to keep it as his own.

Noah had one of his men torch an old barn on his own ranch. Noah rode into town and demanded that the farmer be arrested. He said that the farmer had burned the barn as a way to demonstrate that he didn't want to sell any part of his land and wanted Noah to cease and desist.

Tom had listened carefully and said, "My God, Noah, that's the dumbest story you've ever concocted." When Tom had first pinned on the badge, he'd done all of Noah's bidding, just assuming that the old man would never lie to him. But after a few months, it became clear that Noah made up stories about people he perceived as his "enemies" and had the law take care of them for him. Tom and Noah had never been close but once Tom started refusing to do Noah's dirty work, the relationship cooled even more. These days, Noah sent Tom's kids gifts on their birthdays, and always had a huge dinner for them on Christmas, but, except for that, they had little contact. Tom expected that soon enough, Noah would find some excuse to take his badge away. There'd be no point in fighting him. This was Noah's town and would remain so as long as Noah was alive. All Tom could do then was pack up his family and move on. The alternative was to start doing what Noah wanted him to—and Tom would never do that, no matter the circumstances.

The first thing he needed to do, now that he'd written down the significant names and dates, was to talk to Fargo. And then Liz, see what she had turned up.

He checked the jail cells before he left. The combined stench of sweat, vomit, tobacco, and dirty clothes was so strong it seemed to sear his face. If there was a hell, it probably resembled this—humanity in one of its most self-indulgent moments. There were a lot worse crimes than public drunkenness, true, but when you saw this many drunks crammed into so few cells—it was a damned disgusting sight.

He went up front, told his night deputy where he was headed. The day deputies would arrive in half an hour.

You had to give the bastard credit, Deke Burgade thought. He'd damned near made it. And you also had to thank him. There weren't all that many pleasures to be had on Skeleton Key. But Ross McGinnis had given Burgade one of the few to be had. The stupid bastard had tried to escape.

Burgade was one of those tall, slender men who was stoop-shouldered, skinny-armed, and even a bit limp-wristed. His pale face was bland of feature and wrinkled of skin. The only thing distinctive about him was the pirate-like patch over his right blue eye. That gave him not only a sense of menace but an entrée—at least he thought it did—into the very special club of hard-ass hombres. What Burgade might lack in strength and cunning, he more than made up for in meanness. Everything he did was calculated to prove to himself, his victim, and any onlookers that he was a real man.

Take the way he'd tied Ross McGinnis to the hawthorn tree. He took strips of leather, twisted them tight around the man's wrists, and then poured canteen water on the strips. So that any time McGinnis so much as moved under the lashing whip, he'd force the thorns to eat deeper and deeper into his flesh.

Burgade of the eye patch was no pansy torturer. He was a creative sadist who truly enjoyed his work.

He was also a tireless one.

As the blue jays and the brown thrashers and the painted buntings and the phoebes—songbirds all—began their dawn chorus, Burgade was still at it. He'd been at it since just before four a.m., approximately two hours ago.

Sometimes, he even forgot what he was doing, got so lost in his own thoughts—he had a little gal in Little Rock he got to see twice a month and he was planning his next surprise visit to see her—so it was as if his whip hand was an automatic device.

McGinnis had quit screaming a long time ago, which

meant he was probably unconscious. Burgade hated the ones who sissied out and slumped into unconsciousness right away. He'd had a few who swore at him and mocked him for long stretches of time, pretending that the lashes meant nothing. They called him filthy names, they joked about his eye patch, they told him what they were going to do to him when they figured out a way to get free.

And Burgade loved it. He loved a challenge. Damned right he did. Nothing was more fun than turning these boastful prisoners into sobbing, half-insane pieces of ripped flesh and broken spirit. Oh, how they'd plead, all pride fled. But it didn't do them any good. Burgade of the eye patch had that tireless whip hand and it seemed to grow only more tireless when it was working over the ones who sassed him and made fun of him.

He stopped whipping McGinnis. The man had long ago stopped feeling anything. Coward. Chicken shit bastard. Fainting like that so he could escape the lash. Burgade was sure that he himself could stand up to any kind of whipping anybody could give him.

He went up to McGinnis and looked him over. He always stripped them before whipping them. He lashed every part of their body's back side. From the ankles right up to the crown of the head.

McGinnis was a mess of wounds that were like the mouths of tiny dying children crying out for mercy and help. This bastard wouldn't start feeling good again for a couple of months. And the others, seeing him, sure wouldn't try to escape.

He used the pliers on the wrists, twisting the leather strips free. The tree's thorns had been hungry. Long strings of flesh and blood hung from the tree. On the left wrist you could see bone.

He reached down and dragged McGinnis through a patch of wildflowers, yellow jasmines, orchids, and wild verbenas. The island was not without its beauty.

He dragged McGinnis all the way down to the river and then hauled him face first into the water. If McGinnis died, Burgade would just push the corpse out into the deeper water and let it sink.

If McGinnis was alive, he'd come awake soon enough.

Burgade went back, sat his bony ass on a small boulder,

and watched as McGinnis hung there between life and death for a long, long moment.

The first impression McGinnis gave was that he preferred life. He sputtered and splashed as he tried to raise his head. He even managed to speak a few words. Not that Burgade could understand them.

And then he died.

Or sure gave that impression, anyway.

Just buoyed flat on the surface of the water, unmoving.

Burgade walked to the river and started to wade the corpse into the deeper water. Wanting to be sure that McGinnis really was a corpse, Burgade seized his head, turned him over until he was face up. And then took his hunting knife and cut McGinnis's throat.

A cautious man, Burgade cut the throat a second time, this time using the hunting knife in the opposite direction.

Red blood tainted the blue, blue water.

Burgade went back to the camp and fixed himself some breakfast.

16

Smell of river. Scorch of sunlight. Stab of back pain.

Fargo woke, disoriented.

A stretch of flawless blue sky above him. A snoring Aaron Tillman lying about two feet away from him.

Then he remembered everything.

He lay on the deck of a large, yacht-like boat. They'd been transferred from the wagon some time ago. From what he could see, this was quite a vessel, what they called a well-smack schooner that had been custom-fitted with a mainsail and a smaller sail called a mizzen. There were four oars, two on each side. And a large cabin in the center of the boat. The cabin door faced the port side.

He raised himself slowly and with great pain. A wide stretch of river. And in the sun-splashed, hazy distance he could see land rising abruptly from the water.

He realized he was seeing the infamous island for the first time. The closer they got, the more lush and inviting the island looked. You wouldn't expect that hell could look so good. But Fargo suspected that despite its rugged, natural appeal, the island held secrets dark enough to scare just about anybody.

He allowed himself one of his rare moments of doubt. His plan had been to get on the island and destroy whatever Noah Tillman had set up there. But what if he became just one more of Noah's prisoners, one who couldn't do anything more than submit to whatever Noah demanded. Sometimes, he drew courage from all the tales people told of him. Living up to the legend of the Trailsman inspired him as it inspired others. But he wasn't invincible.

Had he put himself in the middle of a trap from which there was no escape?

Ekert appeared just before the boat reached land. Unshaved, he looked grizzled and tired. He toted a six-gun in one hand and a bottle of whiskey in the other. Even given the pitch of the craft in the choppy water, he staggered more than was necessary.

He went straight to Aaron Tillman, stood over the shackled man sprawled on the deck.

"Morning, Mr. Tillman."

"You sonofabitch. You've been waiting a long time for this, haven't you?" Aaron snapped.

"You notice I called you 'Mr. Tillman,' Mr. Tillman?" Ekert smiled, tilted the bottle up, took a long swig that made his Adam's apple bobble. "You know what your brother was nice enough to let me do?"

Aaron just glared at him.

"He said I could do anything to you I wanted. Anything at all."

The pointed-toe kick of the cowboy boot did maximum damage, caught a rib and cracked it. Aaron screamed and began to twist back and forth in great and immediate pain.

"All the times I had to clean up your puke; all the times I had to haul you out of saloons before somebody killed you because you were such a prick when you were drunk; all the times I had to put you on my shoulder and carry you out of whorehouses because you'd passed out—and you never said thanks. Not even once, Mr. Tillman. You realize that? All those years and you couldn't even bring yourself to say thank you even one time. You said I was scum. Remember all the times you called me that? Called me scum and trail trash? You even spit in my face one time. That's the one that got me. That's the one I can't forget, Mr. Tillman. Spitting on me."

Aaron groaned, cursed, groaned again.

Fargo knew that there was no pain quite like the needle-sharp, insistent ache of a cracked rib. And he'd heard the bone crack loud and clear.

"I don't get to stay on the island with you, Mr. Tillman. But I thought I'd give you the same kind of treatment you gave me all these years."

Fargo knew what was coming; he figured Aaron did, too. But for the moment Fargo listened to all the resentment and hatred in Ekert's voice. He hated Ekert, wanted to kill him. But he had to give the man his dignity—something Aaron in his drunken arrogance had taken from him a long time ago. The weak brothers of strong, powerful men are pretty hard to take under the best of circumstances. He sensed that Aaron had probably been a champion bully.

The second kick was even swifter than the first. And just as devastating. A tad higher up. Another terrible cracking sound. Rib number two.

"You work Daisy over the same way before you killed her?" Fargo said.

Another swig of the bottle. Another grin on the grizzled face. "Now, Mr. Fargo, I sure wouldn't go around hurtin' women this way. Not unless I was paid to do it. And Noah, he paid me to kill her quick and clean. He always tells me how he wants things done. Sometimes he lets me have a little fun, sometimes he don't. Daisy died quick, if that's what you're worried about. I just hope you killed the Mex quick, too. He was a pretty good partner. Now I got to find me a new one."

Short-leaf pines lined the shore. A long, narrow dock extended like a finger into the water. Dogs greeted the approaching boat with violent barks. Killer dogs, no doubt. A short man in a khaki shirt and jeans appeared, toting a shotgun. He waved. Ekert waved back.

A touching scene, Fargo thought. Two killers greeting each other. He wondered again if he'd done the sensible thing, putting himself in such a situation.

Then he decided to hell with it. All this mental jawing was worthless. He was here; it was too late to turn back, and now he needed to spend his time figuring out how to tear the island apart and bring down Noah Tillman in the process. And, oh yes: get his hands on Ekert and beat the sumbitch to death.

The khaki-shirted man walked to the pier, grabbed the rope that was thrown him and helped bring the large craft in true.

Ekert leaned down to Aaron and spat in his face. "I've been waitin' a long, long time for that, Mr. Tillman. I sure have."

A minute later, Ekert stood on the dock with the other man. They were soon off-loading provisions. And then they were off-loading two shackled prisoners, Skye Fargo and Aaron Tillman by name.

Just after eight o'clock, Tom Tillman left the sheriff's office and walked two blocks down to the newspaper office. He did a lot of smiling, even a bit of handshaking, a part of his job as the local enforcer of laws. To a lot of folks hereabout, a lawman was the closest thing they had to a celebrity. There was the mayor, but he didn't carry a gun and didn't go after bad men. And there was a parson and a priest but they didn't carry guns, either, and the only bad men they saw were the kind who filled the pews on Sunday and pretended to be holy, the hypocrites.

The street was packed with revelers. There had to be—or seemed to be, anyway—several hundred thousand tykes from ages three to eleven running, jumping, shouting, screaming, laughing, crying, giggling, hopping, crawling, and whining everywhere he turned. In some ways, he was blessed that the missing persons matter had taken all of his attention. Dangerous as it might prove to be, it was still better than trying to deal with little ones who couldn't find their mommies, drunks who liked to hit people, and traveling thespians who tried to sneak innocent girls into their tents to introduce them to the sweaty miracles of sex.

Liz was alone, sitting at her neatly organized rolltop desk. Two stacks of envelopes sat in front of her. One stack was three times as tall as the other.

She looked up, smiling, when she saw Tom. "Care to guess which one is bills and which one is income?"

"It's a good thing you've got the constitution of a bobcat. You're in one tough business."

She put out her arm. Tom took her hand. She said, "Well, at least I don't get shot at in *my* business."

"You write another one of those editorials saying everybody in the North and the South should calm down and talk reasonably—somebody might shoot you then."

They both knew he was only half-joking. She'd written one such editorial, urging both sides in the increasingly bitter debate over slavery to try to be more civil. The night the editorial appeared, her front window was smashed. Two

97

nights later, somebody set the back of her building on fire. Luckily, a passerby saw the blaze when it was still controllable. It had been put out with minimum damage.

"You're over here mighty early," she said.

They were both careful to avoid any talk of romance, hurt feelings, or sneaking off to see each other. Tom's bearing this morning allowed for none of it. He was able to signal his intentions just by his disposition. Now, he was all business.

"I wanted to find out if Richard ever learned anything about Skeleton Key," he said.

She nodded. "Enough to know that's where our answer must be."

"Exactly. Noah's my stepfather and I still don't know anything about it. He claims it's private because he keeps his best breeding stock there. But the times I've been by it in a canoe, all I ever see is a man standing at a dock with a shotgun."

"What I hear about is those dogs. They've got a legend of their own."

"The fisherman?"

She nodded. "I hope it's just a story."

Anytime you make anything off-limits to the public, you inspire all kinds of tales. Anything secret must be evil. Everybody who'd come within a quarter mile of Skeleton Key had heard the dogs. No doubt that they were merciless killers.

It didn't take long for all sorts of stories to be passed on. The best had to do with voodoo, a boatload of Haitian slaves being transported to Skeleton Key to do some kind of undisclosed work. As the story had it, the slaves naturally enough got tired of being slaves and decided to turn the dogs loose on the masters. To do this, the slaves hoobie-joobied the dogs with some kind of devil hex and the dogs dined on the masters while the slaves slipped away.

According to the same story, the dogs were still hexed, which not only made them dangerous, it also made them immortal. Yes, immortal. As Satan's own, they could not be killed. No poison, ax, spear, or gun could take their lives.

Tom said, "I'm going out there tonight."

"Are you insane?" She was so startled by his comment,

she accidentally knocked over both carefully balanced sets of envelopes with a stray elbow.

"It's the only way. Something's going on on that island. And people have gone missing. Look at it that way, Liz. You have missing people, you have a mysterious island. As a lawman, I have to check that place out and find out what's going on there."

"But the dogs—"

He took her hand. "I don't have any choice. It's my job."

"Then I'm going with you."

He smiled. "Now *you're* the insane one."

"Why shouldn't I go? I run a newspaper. I'm supposed to keep the public informed. So I should be there right along with you."

"But the dogs—"

She grinned. "Huh-uh. That won't work on me, Tom Tillman. I'm just as resourceful as you are. If you're willing to take a chance with those hellhounds, so am I."

"I could always slip away without telling you."

"If you do, Sheriff, I'll be a lot tougher on you than those dogs ever could be."

"You're serious about going?"

"Absolutely. In fact, I'm so serious about going, if you try and stop me, I'll tell everybody I know what you're up to. And word'll get back to Noah and he'll stop you one way or the other."

"But that's blackmail."

"I never claimed to be virtuous, Sheriff. Just hard-working."

It was clear that both of them thought that this could be a pretty good time to slide into each other's arms. You could feel that kind of tension in the air. But it was also clear from the way they were restraining themselves that they weren't about to give in to their impulse. This was business and a damned serious business at that.

"I'll meet you at Simpson's Ridge at nine o'clock tonight," he said.

He tried to keep his voice free of the fear he felt. He just kept thinking of what those dogs could do to a man. Or worse, to a woman.

17

The settlement, such as it was, consisted of two large log cabins made from the wood of the dense forest that comprised ninety-five percent of the island. Additionally, there was a long dog run made of heavy timber, one half of it roofed and sided with wood so the animals could avoid getting soaked when it rained. A tall, rugged post stood in the middle of the clearing. The blood that soaked it indelibly made it obvious that this was the sort of whipping post plantation owners used for their disobedient slaves.

A tall, sinewy man with a bullwhip dangling from his right hand, stood near the whipping post watching as Fargo and Aaron were led, still shackled wrist and ankle, out of the forest and into the clearing.

Burgade said to Ekert, "Couple real fine specimens. Should make Noah pretty happy."

"You know Noah," Ekert said in a sour tone. "*Nothing* makes him happy."

Burgade laughed. "Old Noah gnawing on that bony ass of yours again?"

"You damned right." Then, looking at the cabin to his left: "Them gals in there?"

"Yeah. Sleepin'. I made 'em run all night. Make sure they were all ready for Noah when he gets here."

"He isn't gonna keep 'em anymore, huh?"

A sly grin on Burgade's face. "Nope. They're almost twenty-two. You don't want 'old ladies' like that hangin' around, do ya?"

"They can hang around me all they want."

"Me, too."

Ekert said, "Well, I'll be pushin' off."

"You hate it here, don't you?"

"Place spooks me. I'm always afraid old Noah's gonna put *me* on here someday." He nodded goodbye and started walking away.

Fargo had listened to this with his usual curiosity, trying to figure out what exactly took place on the island. He didn't know for sure. But he was starting to have a hunch and it was a terrifying thought. A man could get jaded when he had as much as Noah Tillman did. It got harder and harder to buy a thrill. Even big game hunting started to pall after a time.

That left only one kind of animal that could make a hunt truly worthwhile.

Fargo had drifted into his own thoughts when the lash of the whip trenched a line of fiery pain across his chest. The tip of the whip held a metal head.

Aaron got the same kind of lash.

"I thought I'd introduce myself," Burgade said. "Deke Burgade. I run this little place for Noah Tillman." He smiled with rotten teeth at Fargo. "I believe you've met him a few times in your travels." He snapped the whip with lurid, dangerous grace. He was obviously impressed with himself and now he meant to impress them, too.

"In case you haven't figured it out yet, Noah comes here to hunt. There's a lot of wildlife in the forest. But he got tired of the same old thing. You know how rich people are, right, Aaron? They always need something new. And that's how he came up with the idea of hunting humans. They present the greatest challenge. So every Fourth of July, Noah comes out here and has himself a real good time."

Aaron said, "He's crazy. This is the most inhumane thing I've ever heard of."

"It may be," Burgade said, "but at least it's fun. There's nothing like hunting people. Noah's let me join the festivities from time to time. And this year, he's throwing the two gals into the mix."

"What gals?" Fargo said.

"Two of the most beautiful sisters you've ever seen. And not just their faces—their bodies, too. They look like something a fella'd dream about."

"Where'd they come from?"

"They was visiting town a couple of years ago and I thought they'd be perfect as a surprise for old Noah. I grabbed 'em myself. Brought them here."

"I'll bet that made them happy."

"You've got a tongue on you, Fargo." He paused. "I take extra special care of them. Noah wants me to. They've got good food, they keep themselves clean in the lake about a quarter mile from here, and they sure get plenty of exercise. Even here they've got their vanity. They know they're beautiful and they want to stay that way. Even if they don't have the freedom they once did."

Fargo nodded to the empty dog run. "Where're the animals?"

Burgade shrugged. "I let 'em roam most of the day. They make sure that nobody comes ashore who isn't supposed to be here."

"I don't suppose anybody's ever escaped from this place," Fargo said.

"Oh, they've tried, Mr. Fargo. In fact, I believe you knew Daisy. Well, the poor girl's brother was here for less than half a day. He tried to escape. Almost made it to the water before Demon and Devil got hold of him."

"Them being two of the dogs, of course."

"Of course, Mr. Fargo."

"This can't go on much longer," Aaron said. "Tom Tillman's already curious about this island. He'll start to investigate."

Burgade smiled. "I don't think old Noah is real worried about *anything* young Tom might do. Tom's a good local lawman. But there's no way he could ever outsmart Noah and get on this island. And until he does that, everything he hears falls into the category of rumor and gossip."

Then he led them to their prison, the one disguised as a friendly-looking log cabin.

Noah Tillman said, "I'll be leaving in a couple of hours, Manuel."

"Yessir."

"I want all my hunting gear laid out. I'll take care of the guns myself."

"Yessir."

Noah laughed. "Maybe I can do better than last year."

"Three men in six hours. I don't know how much better you can get than that. They'd gotten to know the island pretty well."

Last year, Noah had given Burgade permission to set the three men loose in the island for a week in advance. It wasn't difficult to shoot somebody who'd never seen the terrain before. And the more difficult, the better. The prisoners had taken advantage of Noah's largesse. They'd led him a hell of a merry chase. They'd found every cave, every gulley, every tall, lush tree on the island. And then he'd made it even more difficult for himself by limiting his hunting time to six hours. And yet he'd managed to locate and kill every one of them.

This year, given the late arrival time of Fargo and Aaron, he'd instructed Burgade to give them several extra considerations. They probably wouldn't appreciate what Noah was doing for them—making the thing as sportsmanlike as possible—but Burgade thought they were being coddled and treated far too well. But then, when it came right down to it, Burgade was one sadistic sonofabitch.

Now it was time to take down his favorite weapon. He turned from his desk in the study to the large safe in the east rear corner of the spacious room. He had won them two years ago in a crooked poker game in New Orleans. He'd been the crooked one. He knew he could drive Cal Hawkins to desperation—and did. Hawkins was left with nothing to bid other than his most prized possession—even more prized than his wife and children—the weapon he had taken off a Pawnee warrior chief two years earlier. Night Wolf had been one of the most feared warriors in the Oklahoma territory. Until, that is, Hawkins shot him in the shoulder and then cut his throat. The tribe had earlier honored their chief by giving him the gift of a handcrafted seven-shot Spencer carbine that had once belonged to an army captain, a handcrafted carbine sheath and a pair of gloves made of the same leather and beading as the sheath itself. Noah believed that since the carbine had once belonged to such a fierce warrior, it was bound to make him a keener and better hunter.

He stood holding it now with a reverence that was almost mystical. There was still enough little boy in him—in all men—to speculate on what it would have been like to be an Indian warrior in the days before the white man, when such warriors had free reign over the entire country. He could easily picture himself in a loincloth and war paint.

Then, reality returned and he realized what he'd actually be doing tonight.

Killing his own brother.

"It's good to see you holding that rifle, sir. It suits you very well."

Manuel was an ass-kisser, no doubt about that. But for once, Noah fell victim to Manuel's flattery. Noah fancied that the rifle suited him very well indeed.

Incarceration, like death, has its own stench.

There is something about holding men and women against their will that saturates a room with its own odors. You can scrub and clean all you want but the smell remains.

When Burgade led Fargo and Aaron into the log cabin where the prisoners were kept, Fargo was struck by the apparent cleanliness of the place—and the odors that no amount of cleanliness could get rid of.

He was in handcuffs and leg irons.

And so were the two young women who stood before him.

Sun-bleached hair, long, tawny, supple bodies that spoke of strength and animal pleasure, the two girls could easily have been twins—the same azure blue eyes, the same elegantly tilted noses, the same large carnal mouths. And the same full, nipple-hardened breasts that pushed against the work shirts they wore with their jeans.

They appraised Fargo with open lust. These were very lonesome ladies.

"I'm Nancy Tolan," the first woman said. "I'm the oldest by a year. I know we look alike when you first see us but my eyes have some green in them and see this?" She indicated a long white scar that trailed the right side of her jaw. "Stephanie doesn't have a scar. At least not here."

Stephanie laughed. "I'm younger by almost two years. You can tell me because I'm missing half of my little finger." She held up her left hand. Her little finger, as she'd said, had been cleaved clear off. "The first night we were here, Mr. Burgade wanted to show us what a big, strong man he was. So he cut off my finger. I'm sure he's proud of himself. We're sure proud of *him*."

Burgade's tolerance for mockery was low. He crossed to Stephanie and slugged her. Not slapped—slugged, the way he would slug another man in a bar fight.

The astounding thing was that Stephanie absorbed the punch. She might have been rocked back an inch or so on her heels but for the most part she took the punch without moving. Her eyes even showed some slight amusement. She didn't want to give the bully Burgade any pleasure at all.

"Notice how we talk?" Nancy said. "That's Mr. Burgade's idea, too. He makes a monthly trip into New Orleans and spends his time in whorehouses there. He says the girls have a certain way of talking—they always sound like geishas in Japan—always friendly and in awe of the menfolk and eager to do whatever those menfolk want to."

"You want what your sister got, Nancy?" Burgade said.

"I'd rather have that than have you try and rape me again."

Stephanie giggled. "Thank God for alcohol. A lot of men can't get up for the occasion, if you know what I mean."

The women used the only weapon they had. Scorn. They constantly reminded Burgade that he wasn't much of a man if he had to control women by shackling them. And they suggested—or at least their tone did—that someday they might get a chance to pay him back for all the physical pain and degradation he had inflicted on them.

"He's afraid we'll tell poor old Noah that he tried to rape Nancy," Stephanie said. "Poor old Noah wants us kept for himself. He'd kill poor Mr. Burgade if he ever managed to get the job done, right poor old Mr. Burgade?"

So Nancy got what Stephanie had gotten—a balled fist colliding with the front of her lovely face. But like her sister, Stephanie wore the blow like a badge of honor, one more way of demonstrating to Burgade that he might have their bodies in shackles but that he'd never shackled their spirit.

"One of these days, Noah's gonna get tired of you two," Burgade said. "And then he's gonna let me do what I want to you. And that's when I'm gonna cut you both into little tiny pieces."

Stephanie laughed. "You say the sweetest things, Mr. Burgade."

He scowled at them, angry and impotent in the face of their cool contempt.

He then scowled at Fargo and Aaron. "Welcome to Skeleton Key, boys. I'm gonna split you up into teams, one fella, one girl, and then you can explore the island to get used to it."

"What if we try to escape?" Fargo said.

"I'll answer that one for you," Nancy said. "The dogs are trained to kill anybody who approaches the water."

"And Burgade here is the only one who knows the command to make them back down," Fargo said.

"Exactly," Burgade said.

With that, glaring at the women and clearly wishing he could smash them in the face again, he went out slamming the door behind him. Then you could hear him locking it.

"Pig," Nancy said as the crash of the door sent echoes through the walls.

"Someday we'll have *him* in chains," Stephanie said.

Nancy shook her lovely blond hair. "Maybe not, Sis. I think tonight's the night old Noah kills us."

Aaron laughed. "My brother would take great offense at being called 'Old Noah' all the time."

"Well," Nancy snapped, "if it offends you, Mr. Tillman, why don't you get the hell out of here?"

"Go easy on him," Fargo said. "Noah plans to kill him, too."

"You're old Noah's brother?" Stephanie said.

"That's right. And I've been a burden to him most of his life. Tonight he's going to pay me back."

The women went over and sat on their respective bunks. They moved as swiftly as the leg irons would permit.

"You do a good job with those irons," Fargo said.

"Well, after all the time we've spent in them," Nancy said, "we're used to them."

"This place is damned clean," Fargo said, mincing around in his irons. "Can't believe they'd spend so much time on it."

"Believe it or not, old Noah sees that we're fed well, exercised well, and live in pretty nice surrounds." Stephanie reached under her pillow and pulled out the makings. "He wants us to be in good condition when he decides to stalk us through the woods and kill us. More sporting for him that way." She nodded to the tobacco and papers she had. "Anybody want a smoke?"

Both men said yes.

They sat on the cot nearest the ladies.

"You make a mean smoke," Fargo said. Nancy had tucked it in his mouth and lit it for him. The rest he had to do on his own, giving himself a quick lesson in how to smoke while manipulating a pair of tight handcuffs.

"So you know this island pretty well?" Fargo asked.

"Not as well as old Noah and Burgade do," Nancy said.

"Anybody ever survived their hunt?"

"Us. But that's because old Noah decided to keep us around for a while."

"He's a damned good hunter," Aaron said, watching his own cigarette being rolled. "I have to give him that."

"And nobody's ever figured out how to slip past the dogs?" Fargo said.

"They aren't dogs," Nancy said. "They're devils from hell. I know that sounds dramatic but I half suspect it's true. They're a lot craftier than most of the people I know."

"I'd rather be killed by old Noah than by those dogs," Stephanie said.

Nancy said, "We saw a man get ripped apart by them one day. By the time they finished with him, he looked like a side of beef. There wasn't enough of him left together to even tell he was human." She shuddered at the memory.

"They ever threaten to turn on Burgade?" Fargo said.

The ladies thought it over.

"Once, the one named Hellion turned and snapped at him," Nancy said. "Burgade cracked him with the whip across the back. Put a real deep wound in him. That's the closest I've ever seen the dogs getting after Burgade."

"Noah trained those dogs himself," Aaron said. "I couldn't stand to see or hear the way he raised them. He beat them 'til they bled. They were dangerous even when they were puppies, the way he treated them. By now they've got to be crazed. Burgade can't be any better for them than Noah was."

When Aaron got his cigarette, he lay on the fourth cot.

Fargo laid down, too. "We had a long night, ladies. What we need is a little sleep."

Stephanie laughed. "I can think of a couple of things *I*

need, Mr. Fargo." She stared unabashedly at his crotch. Even as exhausted as he was, close proximity to these two made it impossible for his manhood to rest. It bulked up the tight area of his pants.

Nancy was no different. "I was noticing the same thing you were, Sis."

"God, ladies, I really do need a rest."

Aaron rumbled. "I need sleep. How about some silence?"

He rolled over, his back to the three of them.

Both gals stuck their tongues out at him and then grinned at Fargo.

Nancy winked at Fargo. He wasn't sure why but in the next few minutes he learned that Nancy knew her sister very well. Both Stephanie and Aaron fell asleep.

Nancy put a *shhh-ing* finger to her lips and then tiptoed over to him, making as little noise as she could given the situation.

"We'll have to be very quiet," she whispered in his ear.

She began by leading on tiptoes to the east corner of the cabin where he managed to work her jeans down to the middle of her thighs. She faced away from him and was able to spread her legs just enough that Fargo could ease his large and eager rod into the moist and magnificent opening to her womanhood.

He had never before trysted with so many restrictions on him. He couldn't move too quickly or their shackles would make noise. He couldn't speak or moan. And she had all the same restrictions.

But he found it very satisfying. He reached up under her blouse and cupped his hand over one of her breasts, both of them surging when contact was made. And the excitement of this moment helped them find the right pace that both of them could share and enjoy.

He quietly worked himself far up inside her, her round buttocks working against his body, only enhancing his desire. She was able to turn her face so that his tongue could slide into her mouth. The increasing urgency pushed even him further up inside her and her muscles there contracted, driving him to the brink of sanity.

They pressed together so tight that when release came

he fell against her and continued grinding into her. She didn't want to stop and he didn't, either.

Finally they slid to the floor and lay on their backs, a sweaty pile of purely pleased humanity.

Fargo was awakened by the violent barking of the dogs. They'd been barking on and off, but from some distance, so he'd been able to pack in three hours of sleep. But this barking was right outside the door of the cabin. He jerked up from deep sleep, momentarily disoriented.

The sisters and Aaron Tillman were just waking up, too.

"I wish I had a gun," Aaron said grumpily, rubbing sleep from his face. "Right now I'd kill those dogs even before I killed Burgade."

"I don't think you *could* kill those dogs," Nancy yawned. "Even if you had *two* guns. I'm not sure anything could kill them."

Stephanie laughed. "Except maybe Burgade's breath."

"Now there's a weapon I hadn't thought of," Nancy said.

Fargo admired the dialogue. Most prisoners would have long ago—and understandably—sunk into depression and silence. You could only live like this so long before captivity broke you physically and spiritually. But the sisters' bright chatter spoke of their bravery and determination to survive this experience.

Burgade came in. "Aaron and Stephanie. You're going out first. Walk over here now."

"Maybe it'd be easier if you'd just shoot us right here and get it over with," Aaron said.

"That'd be fine with me. But your brother wouldn't get his fun if I did that. And one way or another, we all need to keep your brother happy. Now shut your stupid mouth and get your ass over here."

Fargo watched as the shackled couple made their way to Burgade who stood frowning and impatient, his rifle cradled in his arms as if it were his infant.

When they reached him, Burgade handed Stephanie a key and said, "Take the shackles and cuffs off both of you and then give me the key back."

"You're not afraid we might jump you?" Aaron smiled.

"First of all, you haven't got the guts. Second of all, this rifle would cut you in half at this range. And third of all, even if you got past me, the dogs are right outside." And right on cue, the dogs started barking again, sounding both vicious and hungry.

Stephanie unlocked the shackles and the cuffs and handed the key to Burgade, who then went to the door and whispered three words in Indian dialect that silenced the dogs instantly. Fargo was impressed. The sonofabitch not only spoke so low it was just about impossible to hear him; he also spoke in what sounded like an Indian tongue Fargo had never heard before.

Burgade waved his rifle at Aaron and Stephanie. "Outside."

"Those dogs're settled down now?" Aaron asked, obviously afraid.

Burgade grinned. "I guess you'll find out soon enough, won't you?"

They went outside. The dogs didn't bark. Nor did they attack. You could hear Burgade laying out the plan for exploring the island.

But Fargo wasn't paying much attention. He was too busy thinking of ways you could escape dogs whose sole purpose was to kill on command.

18

While his deputies circulated among the crowds on this Fourth of July afternoon, Tom Tillman spent his time asking questions. He made them as subtle as he could, as if he really wasn't asking questions at all but just sort of passing the time. But at least one person must have gotten suspicious about his queries because at around four o'clock a seldom-seen sight appeared like an apparition in the front doorway of the sheriff's office. Noah Tillman himself.

Tom was manning the front desk so he could help folks who stopped in looking for help. Kids got lost, old people got sick from the heat, honest folks inevitably got cheated by various small-time confidence men who always worked crowds like this. And on and on. Tom wanted people to have a good impression of the town so he was as hospitable and patient as he could be.

When Noah saw him there he said, "You shouldn't be sitting out here, Tom."

"Oh? Why's that?"

The coldness of the exchange said a lot about their feelings toward each other. They hadn't liked each other for a long time. And each deeply distrusted the other. They spoke like rivals who had to work together rather than like father and adopted son.

"Now you should be smart enough to figure that out, Tom."

"Go ahead and tell me, Noah. I guess I'm too stupid to understand things most of the time."

Noah sighed. "I didn't come here to argue, son." He always called him son when he wanted to cut the tension. "And all I meant was that since you're the high sheriff, you shouldn't be doing a deputy's work. It doesn't look right for the sheriff to be sitting right out front."

Tom had to smile. Noah's pride was so excessive it was comical. He was always aware of everybody's status. And he sure didn't want his son, even his adopted son, to be doing the lowly work of a deputy.

"What can I do for you, Dad?" Tom didn't try to disguise the ironic tone of "Dad." Noah had never been a father. He'd just never quite taken to the lad and the lad in turn, after several years of trying, decided that he would never take to his adoptive father, either.

Noah took a seat. He took off the fancy straw hat he was wearing and fanned himself. "It's a hot one."

"It sure is."

"The town sure looks nice. Be sure and tell the mayor I think he outdid himself this year."

"You ever going to get around to telling me why you're really here?" He hesitated and then added, "Dad."

"You've got a tongue on you like your mother's. She was always tryin' to cut me down, too."

"Maybe she was just trying to make you tell the truth for once."

Noah stared at him. "You're an ungrateful bastard, you know that? All I've done for you. All that my name got you."

Tom rolled himself a cigarette while Noah threw out some more accusations and grief. After he lit his cigarette, Tom said, "Somebody told you I've been asking questions today about Skeleton Key. That's why you're here, isn't it?"

"What the hell right do you have to go around snooping into my private business?"

"There's a rumor that some people have disappeared. Skeleton Key always comes up. There are a lot of rumors about it."

"Rumors? Hell, Tom, haven't you figured it out by now? When you're rich and powerful the way I am, everybody resents you. And so they start rumors. I once heard that I used to have carnal knowledge of sheep. And don't smile, boy. That was a very serious rumor for a while." He shook his head. "Skeleton Key is a perfectly innocent place. If you want to know, I go there to relax. Nobody gets to pester me there. Including all our relatives who're always asking me for financial help."

"If it's so innocent, why all the secrecy?"

"No secrecy, Tom. No secrecy. The island's there. I'm there. Everybody knows that. That's no secret."

"If it's that innocent, how about letting me look it over?"

Noah scowled. "Hell, no. Why should I? Aren't I entitled to a little privacy?" But he didn't wait for an answer. "Damned right I am. And I intend to keep it, too."

"Then the gossips'll keep on whispering."

"Let 'em whisper."

"Then you're saying you don't know anything about these disappearances?"

Noah frowned. "You may hate me—and I suspect you do—but do you really believe I'd have something to do with people disappearing? Some kind of white slavery ring or something? Is that what you've got in mind?"

"It was a fair question."

"And I gave you a fair answer."

Noah stood up. Winced. "Damned arthritis." He glared at Tom. "I've got spies everywhere, Tom. People may not like me much but they protect me. Because when they protect me, they protect themselves, their jobs, and this peaceable town and the future for their children. So they don't appreciate anybody, including my own adopted son, tryin' to snoop into the little privacy I have in life."

"So you wouldn't like it if I asked some more questions?"

Noah jabbed a finger at him. "I got you this job. You don't remember that. But I did. And you know why I did? Because I figured you'd be good at it. And you are. You're the smartest lawman we've ever had here. And from what I hear, you're also fair. Even the people who don't care for you say that. Say that you don't play favorites. They also say you're not mean, the way some lawmen are."

Noah started walking to the door. "But you know what? Quick as you got that badge of yours, I could take it away. I could go over to a town council meeting and ask for a private session and then I'd lay out some charges against you—tell them that I hated to do this, you being my stepson and all—and you know what? You'd be out of a job within an hour. They'd find some law on the books that made you ineligible to be sheriff anymore. And you'd be out on your ass."

"I take it that's a threat?"

A look of frustration twisted Noah's face. "All I'm saying, boy, is that you're doing a good job. Most people like you. You could have a great future. But just let this island thing go. Forget about it. There's sure a hell of a lot of other work to do, isn't there? You can just quit wasting your time on rumors. Because there's nothing to them." He opened the door. It seemed impossible. The office got even hotter in the few seconds the scorching, dusty wind blew in. A look of reason on his face now. "There's not one damned thing to those rumors, son. Not one damned thing."

Noah left.

And now Tom knew for sure that something terrible was going on out there on Skeleton Key. Otherwise the old man wouldn't have made such a fuss about it.

Liz took down the dagger that had been her husband's pride. The blade was five inches long, the hilt burnished cooper with a cross carved on the handle. They'd bought it in St. Louis soon after they were married. It was said to have been blessed by the Pope in Italy, where it was crafted. Because of the blessing, the shopkeeper explained, no harm would come to anybody who carried it.

Richard always took it along when he knew that a situation was going to be risky. It had kept him safe. But the night he'd been killed, he'd had no reason to take it along. While he was looking into Skeleton Key, at that particular time he was just doing his regular work. No reason to think he'd be ambushed.

She pressed the dagger to her breast now, in sweet memory of her husband. Tom was so much like him. She was blessed that she'd found two such men in her life.

Now that she was home for the day, she began preparing for tonight. She'd wear brown butternuts and a black shirt. She'd cinch her hair back so that it wouldn't get in the way. And she'd carry a handgun—and the dagger with the special blessing.

Even on Skeleton Key, the dagger would keep her alive. She was sure of it.

19

Fargo said, "Any caves on this island?"

"Two or three," Nancy said. "But they aren't very big. We thought of that, too. But the dogs would find us right away and kill us."

Fargo smoked his cigarette. Aiming the smoke in a narrow stream at the rough hewn roof of the log cabin. "You ever notice any place in the forest where water backed up in a real small area?"

"Can't think of any place offhand. Why?"

"Sometimes islands have underground passages that lead to the water. I got trapped in a place like this once before. This Apache I was with got us free that way."

"I wish I could think of something like that."

"And you never heard of any way of tricking those dogs?"

"Are you kidding? They couldn't be tricked by anybody. They want to kill people. That's all they think about. Even when they're sort of lazing in their dog runs, the way they watch you—" She shook her head. "They're the scariest things I've ever run up against, Fargo."

Fargo was quiet for a time. She was probably right. Even if the dogs weren't invincible, a man couldn't outrun them. About all he could do was shoot them, which was hard to do if you didn't have a gun.

The underground stream had been one idea. What were others? He wondered. He closed his eyes. Tried to picture the glimpse of the forest he'd gotten on his way in here.

He studied the mental picture carefully. The dock was out. So was any shoreline. And Nancy had ruled out caves as a place to hole up and avoid getting killed. If a man got lucky, he might be able to find the right kind of rock to

115

crush a dog's head with. The trouble with that was, even if you managed to ultimately kill the dog, the toll on the man would be considerable. Might lose an arm or a leg. He might kill the dog—and get himself killed in the process.

That left one possibility: the trees. There might be a way that you could find trees strong enough that you could cross them, one to another, at their very tops. It would take time, skill, and most of all luck. But right away you'd eliminate the danger of the dogs. And Noah and Burgade would have a hell of a time shooting you if you were up high enough and constantly moving among heavily leafed branches.

"What're you thinking, Fargo?"

"Just running through ideas."

"I'm glad they captured you."

"Thanks."

"I'm being selfish, I know. But the other men they kidnapped and brought here—you mentioned Daisy. All her brother could do was taunt Burgade, which wasn't smart. Then he got dumb enough to try and race the dogs to the water. You've never seen anything uglier than what those dogs did to him." She leaned across from her cot to his and kissed him on the mouth. "I'm sorry I said that I'm glad they captured you. I'm just glad we've got a man here finally who's got some ideas."

"Just because I've got the ideas doesn't mean that they'll work out."

"Well, at least you're not thinking of racing the dogs to the water."

He frowned. "Poor bastard. He must've been pretty desperate."

"He was more worried about his sister than he was himself. I'll say that for him. That's why he had to get off the island he told us—to save his sister before they found her and killed her."

The new picture in his mind was the face of Ekert. The Trailsman owed Ekert a death—his own. And the same for Noah. How degenerate, how jaded, how perverted could you get—hunting your own species as sport. You didn't even have the excuse of war. You were just having a good time. He owed Noah Tillman a death, too—and he was damned well going to pay off.

"I'm going to get a little more shut-eye," he said. "Maybe by then they'll be back and it'll be our turn."

"Maybe we can get Burgade's rifle from him and blow his ugly face off."

Fargo grinned. "You're my kind of woman."

They left late in the afternoon, Burgade, the dogs, and Nancy and Fargo. Burgade had given Nancy the key and she'd unshackled both herself and the Trailsman.

It was funny how serene the place was, Fargo thought, when you looked straight ahead and forgot about the rifle and dogs at your back. Most of the island was land that was untouched by white men. No timber had been chopped. No trenches dug. No shanties or shacks erected. Pure wild forest. And at this time of day, with the sun beginning to sink, there was a sense of completion, as if all the animals and birds were knocking off work after a hard day in the woods.

The illusion of tranquility was ended soon when Fargo heard Nancy curse. She pointed to a pile of bones just off the trail. Human bones long ago picked clean by various animals—whatever small pieces of meat the dogs had been too sated to eat themselves.

"Good old Burgade and his filthy dogs," she said. She didn't cringe from the sight. It obviously just reminded her all over again of how much she hated Burgade. She was a tough woman. No tears. Just rage. Fargo liked that.

Trees soared to the sky. Gnarled, clinging, tangled vegetation covered everything off the path they were traveling. The air was thick with the scents of wildflowers and mint leaves and loam. Butterflies and small birds of brilliant hues soared and dove in play. At a glance, there seemed to be a dozen places that looked like good spots to hide. But this was illusory. The dogs would find you instantly.

To the north were limestone cliffs, to the south a valley that stretched almost the entire width of the island. The valley was covered with a colorful variety of vegetation. What intrigued Fargo was how close its far perimeter was to the water. His eyes searched for trees. If you could elude the dogs by climbing a tree and then diving from a tree into the water.

But life was rarely that simple. No trees grew along this particular stretch of shoreline. You would still have the

117

problem of trying to outrace the dogs to the water. And you'd lose.

When they reached a tiny clearing, Burgade planted his ass on a small boulder and said, "Go on ahead and look around all you want. I need to keep my strength for tonight. Noah always likes me to go along with him. I'll send the dogs along to keep you company."

The dogs.

Fargo wasn't sure what cross-mixture of breeds they were exactly. They were the size of adult greyhounds but their coats were shiny black. Their eyes were a faintly ruby color. Easy to see why the sisters called them demons. Cold, silver spittle constantly dripped from their long snouts and the low rumble in their chest cavities was ceaseless. What struck Fargo most about the dogs was their lack of personality. Play had been trained out of them; and so had most other kinds of dog pleasures, including affection for humans. They were machines and nothing more, their behavior dictated by their trainer and master.

They set off without Burgade.

In the next forty-five minutes, Nancy showed him the caves she'd mentioned, the one possibility that just might be an underground stream, but wasn't, and then a variety of places where they might lie in ambush and turn the tables on Noah and Burgade. The trouble again being the dogs. They might knock out or even kill Noah and Burgade with rocks but the animals would still be there.

He spent a third of their time near the shoreline inspecting the trees. Because the birches were so close together, they offered the fastest escape route. You could use two trees at the same time if you needed to, thereby insuring not only speed but relative safety from falling. The other trees he saw were too thick or too flimsy. What the birches lacked was the heavy leafing of some of the other trees. It wouldn't be easy to hide at the top of them. But then, he decided, no matter which kind of tree they elected, the dogs could sniff them out, anyway. What they'd have to do was reach the top of the trees and then start climbing from tree top to tree top until they reached trees whose leaves would hide them adequately.

And then what? Fargo wondered. He hadn't thought beyond finding a hiding place. But if they could put themselves in a place that would keep them away from the dogs, at least there'd been the hope of surviving the night. Maybe some turn of good luck, some unexpected opportunity might save them.

"You look sort of devious, Fargo," Nancy joked.

"Just part of my personality," he smiled. "Being devious."

"You see any way to avoid getting killed tonight?"

"I'm working on it."

"My sister and I always act like it never gets to us. Being on this island, I mean. We made a pact when we were kidnapped that we'd keep our spirits up. But now that I know we're probably going to die tonight—"

He slid his arm around her. "Don't think about it."

"Is that how you handle it? Not being scared?"

"Who says I'm not scared? But I'm sure as hell not going to give up without a fight."

She slid out from under his comforting arm. "There. That's exactly what I needed. A little kick in the behind to get me going again. I'm mad—I'd like to tear Burgade apart with my hands—and I plan to stay mad." She made fists, serious ones. Fargo had no doubt that she could throw a solid punch. "Now, tell me what's going on in that devious mind of yours."

"How are you at climbing trees?"

"Well, Steph and I were pretty much tomboys when we were growing up. We could outrun, out punch and out climb every boy in our little town. The ones who were our age, anyway. Why?"

"Because that's what I'm working on."

He gave her his theory about how climbing the trees would keep the dogs at bay for a while and might just give them time to figure out a way to kill Noah and Burgade.

"I like all this, Fargo. But you haven't figured out what to do about the dogs yet. I mean, we get down from the tree. And there they are, waiting for us. Then what?"

"That's the part I'm still working on."

"Well," she said, "you'd better work fast."

20

The supper was downright delicious. Slices of beef, baked potato, green beans. Real restaurant repast. Even the dishes the meal was served on were of café quality.

"I told you they fed us well," Stephanie said.

Burgade had left them all unshackled. He joked that it was the least he could do since they were going to be dead in a few hours.

They ate in an empty corner of the log cabin. Sitting on the floor.

"Maybe he put something in the food," Aaron said.

"Like what?" Fargo asked.

"You know, some kind of herb or something that'll slow us down tonight when we're trying to escape my dear brother Noah and his dogs. I sure wouldn't put it past him."

They all looked at their food.

"Thanks, Aaron," Nancy said. "I was actually enjoying this food until you said that."

"Yeah, thanks Aaron," her sister said in the same sarcastic tone.

"Well, we might as well enjoy it," Fargo said, "being that we've all eaten at least half of our meals."

Aaron frowned. "You know, my friend, your optimism could get me down. We're probably less than three hours from our death and you're making jokes."

"Well, there won't be any time for jokes after we die, Aaron. We might as well tell 'em now."

Nancy, trying to alleviate the sudden tension, "Tell him about the trees, Fargo."

"Yes, and while you're at it, tell me about the birds and bees, too." He laughed. "Sorry I got so cranky there, Fargo.

All the times in my miserable life I thought I wanted to die but when I come right up against it—I really want to live. I've got a bad case of nerves." He nodded to Nancy. "I hope our beautiful young companion means that you've got some foolproof escape plan."

"If I had a foolproof escape plan, I'd already be gone," Fargo said.

He went over his plan. He'd added a new angle since talking about it to Nancy. "Since we don't have any weapons, we talked about pelting them with rocks. Maybe knocking them out."

"Or killing the bastards," Stephanie said.

"Right," Fargo laughed, "or killing the bastards if you happen to be as bloodthirsty as Stephanie. But now I've added to the idea. What if we set them up for a trap. Maybe hitting them with rocks would work then."

"How do we set up a trap?" Aaron said. "They've got the dogs and the guns."

"They give us a head start, I hear."

"Fifteen minutes," Stephanie said. "They're so generous."

"All right. So what if we try this?" Fargo said. "We know where the tree branches are thickest with leaves. What if I run on ahead of you three, pick out a tree, carry as many rocks as I can up with me, and then start firing at them as soon as they reach the tree."

"What makes you think they'll stop at that particular tree?" Aaron said.

"You're going to lead them there. You're going to make all the noise you can and they're going to come after you. Then you start scrambling up the birches before they get to me. When they get there, they'll be confused, wondering where you folks are. Then I hit them with the rocks."

"They'll kill you," Nancy said.

"All they'll have to do is point their rifles up there and start blasting away," Stephanie said. "Even if they can't see you, they're bound to hit you eventually."

"I appreciate your concern, ladies, but I don't see that we have much choice."

"You're a braver man than I am," Aaron said.

"That wouldn't take a whole hell of a lot," Nancy said.

"I'm a lot younger and spryer than Aaron here. If he

was my age, I'm sure he'd do it. So let's not go calling each other names."

"I'm sorry, Aaron," Nancy said. "That was a mean thing to say. I guess I've got a bad case of nerves, too."

"Apology accepted. And I agree with you, Nancy. Even if I was Fargo's age, I doubt I'd have the nerve for what he's proposing."

"I'm more than proposing it," Fargo said. "I'm going to do it. And for what it's worth, it's not going to be all that simple for you, either. You've got to scramble up those trees before the dogs get a scent of you."

"I hadn't thought of that," Stephanie said.

"I had," Nancy said. "But I'd rather run our risk than Fargo's." She reached over and touched his arms. "Poor Fargo's going to have two guns blazing away at him."

Fargo watched the preparations from the cabin window. Noah had arrived a half hour ago, carrying one hell of a fancy Spencer. He wore black clothes and his face was smudged with some kind of grease that made his face half as dark as his clothes. From what Fargo could see, the man had also rubbed the same stuff on his hands. Mr. Invisible, Fargo thought. He knows the island a hell of lot better than we ever will. He's got his gunny Burgade, his dogs, and his disguise. Bastard doesn't give us much of anything. It's a poker game of the worst kind—Noah took all the aces out before the game started and shoved them right into his own five cards.

There was a half-moon. The light was unnaturally bright.

Burgade appeared. He had a hunting rifle and a pair of field glasses. Fargo wasn't sure that, even with the brilliance of the moon, the field glasses were going to be a whole lot of help once they got into the forest.

They talked for maybe fifteen minutes, just the two of them, about halfway up from the dock. The dogs weren't barking but they were growling. Tonight just might be their dream—atrocity heaven for carnivores of the worst sort. Even if they could only bag one human, that would be a truly sumptuous and memorable meal. As long as they didn't kill each other fighting over who got the last few bites.

Burgade went over and let the dogs out.

It was sort of funny the way Noah jerked backwards a bit when the animals came out of their run. So the old man was just as afraid of the dogs as everybody else was. Someday, if Fargo could survive the night, that would make one hell of a saloon story.

The dogs got excited with no warning and for no reason Fargo could see. They leapt up at Noah, who kept backing away and did his own sort of barking at Burgade. Even from here, Fargo could see the strain on Burgade's face. He liked to boast about the kind of control he had over the dogs but at moments like these his face told the truth. You could see the fear and the desperation as he began to command the dogs into settling down. At one point, Noah raised the Spencer. He looked as if he were about to shoot one or two of the dogs himself.

Noah broke away abruptly from Burgade and the dogs and stalked to the cabin. He threw the door back and swaggered inside.

"Been looking forward to this for a long time," Noah said to Aaron.

"I may surprise you, brother, and live out the night."

"The only thing that would ever surprise me," Noah said, "is if you sobered up once and for all and got some backbone."

Aaron's expression wasn't exactly inscrutable. Noah's words had hurt and embarrassed him in front of the others. Aaron had apparently found a strange kind of freedom in the cabin. Without Noah around to taunt him, Aaron had been able to pass himself off as a decent, productive human being. But no more. Noah was here to remind him of all his past sins.

"You're coming with me, Aaron."

"I'd rather go with my friends."

Noah smirked. "Friends. These people are riffraff, same as you, Aaron. They'd sell you out in a minute. Ask them. If I offered to set them free and get off this island only if it meant killing you, they'd do it in a second."

"Don't be too sure of that," Fargo said.

"They speak bravely like Fargo here, Aaron," Noah said. "But look at their faces. Do you really think they'd sacrifice themselves for you?"

"That doesn't mean they're not friends of mine," Aaron said.

Fargo saw the vicious way Noah ruled over his brother. Aaron's drinking problem had left him with no self-respect. Aaron obviously agreed with everything Noah said. And Noah said everything. He even mocked the notion that Aaron could have any friends.

"How about it?" Noah said. "What if I seriously offered you a deal like that? I get to kill Aaron here and you three get off the island safely? Would you go for that?"

Nancy's contempt for the old man sounded clear and deep in her voice. "He's your brother. Doesn't that mean anything to you? Your own flesh and blood?"

"Maybe you wouldn't say that if you'd had to take care of him the way I have. Aaron always makes it sound as if he's the wronged one. But given everything I've had to do for him, he should appreciate which of us is really getting the short end of the stick. And now I'm going to do both of us the favor of ending his misery."

He moved without any warning whatsoever. Grabbed Aaron by the arm, shoved him toward the door. He said, "I'm locking you in so don't try to help. I thought we'd get this night off to a good start." He smiled at Aaron. "For once my brother's going to be an asset instead of a liability."

"Please," Aaron said, imploring the others with his eyes and voice. "Please don't let him do this."

Fargo started toward Noah but the old man clipped off a shot that missed Fargo's head by no more than an inch. "I really wanted to save you 'til later, Fargo. You'll be the toughest of these people to hunt down. And therefore you'll be the most fun."

Stephanie had teared up. You could hear her tears in her voice. "He's your damned brother, Noah. You say he was hard to put up with. Maybe so. But when he's sober, he's a decent man. He doesn't deserve this."

"Maybe I was wrong, Aaron. Maybe you really have made some friends here." Noah shook his head in mock sorrow. "Poor Aaron. Everything always happens too late to do him any good."

"You kill him," Fargo said, "I'll kill you."

Noah said, "Now that's the kind of spirit I like to see, Mr. Fargo. You're going to be damned tough in those woods. And that's just going to make everything all that much better for me."

Noah put the tip of his rifle against his brother's head.

Aaron was becoming paralyzed with dread at what was coming next. "You can't do this, Noah. Not even you. I'm your brother."

"Outside," Noah said. "And I mean right now."

Fargo was trying to puzzle out what Noah had in mind here. Not a run through the woods. Aaron wouldn't be much fun as quarry. He'd probably collapse after the first few minutes on the trail.

The door slammed. Fargo heard a key turning in the lock.

Then he heard the dogs barking in a different way. As if Noah was holding food out to them—and then pulling it back. Teasing them.

Then he was at the window with the women, seeing all too clearly what Noah had in mind for his brother.

21

Liz and Tom Tillman set off in an old canoe. They put in outside of town so nobody would see them—hopefully not, anyway.

Liz thought of how romantic an evening like this could be. The croaking of frogs, the song of nightbirds, the silver brilliance of moonlight, the dark majesty of the trees on the shore, the scent of the river cooling off after the day's heat. Just drifting on the water, not caring about what time it was or where they were going. For a moment some of her old guilt came back. Liz had always been true to her husband. She'd been a virgin on their wedding night and she'd never once cheated on him in any way.

She'd had some trouble when she and Tom started seeing each other. He was married for one thing. She made him do the right thing. She made him ask his wife for a divorce. His wife said no. These days Tom slept alone on a cot in their spare room. The marriage was in name only. Beyond that, there was the matter of staying true to her husband. At first, her guilt had paralyzed her, nearly destroyed her relationship with Tom. Here she was enjoying romance and her poor husband Richard was dead in the ground. She'd gotten past it for the most part but it had taken time and a lot of reassurance from Tom that it was the proper thing for her to do. Richard would've gone on with his life, Tom had reasoned; and so should you.

But tonight, vestiges of her guilt returned. She was glad they were going to Skeleton Key, resuming the work that had cost Richard his life. She felt a connection to Richard again, which was good; and in case Richard happened to be in heaven looking down, he'd see that Tom had taken it upon himself to help finish Richard's work for him.

"I still wish you'd wait in the canoe."

"Bring strong man. Leave weak little woman behind."

"You know I don't think of you as a weak little woman."

"Then prove it by not bringing it up any more. I'm going on the island with you and that's that."

"This is probably all moot," Tom said. "I doubt we'll be able to get on the island, anyway. Not with those dogs."

"It's so twisted."

"What is?"

"Raising dogs to be killers. They're born innocent and then some sick bastard perverts their whole nature."

"You wouldn't have a guard dog?"

"If I needed one, sure," she said. "But I wouldn't train it to kill except in extreme circumstances—and then just to protect me. Not to kill for the sport of it."

"I guess I'd have to agree with you there."

For his part, Tom had begun to wonder if going to the island was such a good idea, after all. Noah had become something of a madman over the past ten years. He'd always been angry, willful, and devious. But the way he nurtured his hatreds these days, and the elaborate ways he paid his enemies back. . . . Would Noah kill a woman and his own stepson?

He knew why Liz was here. She was doing this for her husband. And he understood and admired that. But she didn't seem to understand the extreme danger they were in. They didn't have any real idea of what awaited them on the island. They knew about the dogs, but what else might Noah have concocted? They also knew, or at least suspected, that he brought live people to the island. People who never returned. But how did they die? Was it the dogs or something even worse?

"You're having second thoughts, aren't you?" Liz asked softly.

He was always honest with Liz. He didn't need to play the brave, tough sheriff. "Yeah, I guess I am."

"So am I," she said. "So am I."

Noah commanded two of the dogs to attack and two to sit by and watch.

The attackers launched themselves like spears, lean, perfectly balanced, sure of their trajectory. There was little detail to what could be seen of them now. They were blurs more than defined animals.

Aaron had only seconds to try to escape, and that was hopeless. As if the situation wasn't dangerous enough, he managed to trip over his own feet and fall to the ground. The dogs adjusted their aim exactly, slamming into him with such force that his entire body bounced off the hard earth.

And then began the vivisection. Three skilled surgeons working at the same time and with the most deadly sharp scalpels available could not have done the damage the two animals did in the first few seconds of their attack. One animal concentrated on Aaron's head and upper torso. The other took everything below.

Blood, bone, pieces of clothing soaked with blood—all gleamed in the moonlight. When Aaron raised a hand for help, you could see that three of his fingers had already been ripped away.

Barely a minute had elapsed since the attack had begun.

Fargo ran to the door, began slamming himself into it. At this point, he was as crazed as the dogs. He had no idea how he could help the man. But he couldn't stand by and watch all this.

By this time, Nancy was screaming and Stephanie was sobbing and covering her face with her hands. The pitch of her sobs became so shattering that Nancy brought her close in a nurturing hug.

Nancy had already noted that the other two witnesses—Noah and Burgade—were watching the evisceration calmly. Burgade was even dragging on a cigar. They might have been spectators at a side show attraction.

Fargo continued to hurl himself at the door. On his ninth attempt, a shot rang out and a large hole was ripped two inches from his head.

Fargo dove away from the door. Three other shots followed, one on the other. Obviously, Noah didn't want to be distracted from the bloody spectacle taking place in front of him. Fargo just might get lucky, and break through first. He was strong enough. Best to use a few bullets to dissuade him.

Fargo scrambled to his feet and went to the window. The dogs' faces and bodies alike glistened with Aaron's blood.

"He's dead," Fargo said. "At least that's something." He turned away from the window. The rest would be nothing more than watching the animals feasting on dead meat. Fargo was intrigued to see that the two dogs who'd been forced to sit aside were getting more and more difficult for Burgade to control. Audible commands were no longer enough. He had to lash them both with the tip of his bull-whip. They glared at him with the same crazed and frenzied eyes as the two animals now ripping Aaron's flesh from Aaron's bones.

"Noah's insane," Nancy said, leading the trembling Stephanie to a corner, where she sat her down. Stephanie had quit sobbing but her hands were still over her face. How tempting to slip away into the fantasy worlds of the people who lived in asylums. And never have to face the brutality of the real world ever again.

Now, they waited.

Noah loved to keep people off guard. Knowing this, Fargo figured that they wouldn't come for him and the women right away. Noah would let the tension build. Not enough to see them die in the most savage way possible. He had to let the terror build beforehand. Let them know bowel-freezing fear and dread. Let them know true despair. And then come with an abruptness that was almost as brutal as the dogs themselves.

And let the games begin.

The ultimate game.

Man hunting man in a forest filled with dangers of its own.

22

Burgade was the one who noticed that the dog he called Voodoo was acting strangely. While the other dogs sat close together, waiting on Noah's command, Voodoo sat off by himself making odd noises and looking in the direction of the dock.

Burgade knew the dogs better than he knew any human being. For Voodoo to be upset like this, something must be troubling him. Voodoo was the smartest of the dogs. Burgade always paid attention to him.

Noah stood over what was left of his brother. Pieces of entrails were everywhere in the dust. The dogs had succeeded—not without some difficulty—in separating Aaron's head from his shoulders. The head, or what was left of it, lay on the edge of the clearing, seeming with its one eye to observe everything that was going on.

Burgade walked over to Noah and said, "They did a good job."

"It's a terrible thing when a man doesn't feel anything for his own brother," Noah said.

Burgade naturally assumed that Noah—even cold old Noah—was having doubts about having his brother ripped apart by the dogs.

"I don't think he ever appreciated one damned thing I did for him," Noah said. "The only thing he ever cared about was himself. Selfish bastard."

Burgade fought a smile. He should have known that Noah wouldn't have any regrets. He wasn't talking about what he'd done to Aaron, he was talking about what Aaron had done to him. Nice to know there was something stable in the world—Noah's unforgiving heart. Not even Burgade could have looked down at the pieces of his brother and not felt regret. But Noah? No problem.

"Voodoo's agitated," he said to Noah.

"That dog's always agitated."

"I want to take him down around the dock. See if anybody's tried to sneak onto the key here."

Noah pointed his Spencer at the cabin. "I want to start the hunt."

"But what about Voodoo?"

"To hell with Voodoo. Someday I'm going to shoot that noisy bastard and replace him."

The thought of shooting one of the dogs did not sit easily with Burgade. His special, if violent, relationship with them made him not only their trainer but protector as well. Yes, funny as it sounded, the dogs needed protection too—shelter, food, and safety from the whims of their crazy old owner, Noah Tillman.

"Don't look at me like that," Noah snapped. "Every time I say something about one of those damned dogs, you look like you're ready to shoot me in the back."

Not a bad idea, Burgade thought.

Noah sighed. "Dammit, I want to get going on the hunt." He made a face. "All right. Take Voodoo and check things out. But I want you back here in ten minutes."

Burgade made a special sound. His Voodoo-only call. The other dogs growled now as they saw Voodoo trot over to their master.

"I won't be long," Burgade said as he set off.

"You damned well better not be."

Actually, Burgade was thankful for this respite from Noah. Even though his boss hadn't been here long tonight, the tension and resentment Burgade always felt toward the old man was already rolling in his stomach.

"You going to be all right with them? Alone I mean?" Burgade said.

Noah sneered. "Why the hell wouldn't I be? I'm the one that bought them in the first place, wasn't I? I was the one that trained them before you came along, wasn't I? Why the hell *wouldn't* I be all right with them? They'll take my command over yours any day, Burgade. And if you think they won't, let's just try it sometime. These dogs are mine, not yours."

"I was just—"

"Now get the hell going. And get back here right away. This Fargo isn't going to be easy. This just might be the best hunt I've ever had. And I'm not going to let you and Voodoo spoil it for me. You understand, Burgade?"

Burgade nodded.

"Good. Now get your ass out of here."

As Burgade started to set off, the other dogs started barking with great resentment at Voodoo. He hunched low and growled.

Let Noah be the master of the other three dogs. Burgade would be happy to settle for Voodoo. Burgade glanced back at the cabin, glimpsed Fargo's face in the window. One thing Noah was right about, for sure. Fargo was going to give them a lot rougher time than anything ever had.

He was going to be one nasty sumbitch.

Fargo said, "Take off your clothes."

"What?" Nancy said.

"Only chance we've got."

He explained quickly. She agreed without hesitation, slipping out of her jeans and shirt to reveal the curves and hollows and swells of flesh that he had known all too recently. In the moonlight, she looked pale and ethereal, her dark eyes, her naturally red lips, and the explosion of black pubic hair the most vivid parts of her now.

Fargo grabbed a chair. Dragged to the spot in front of the door.

"I'm going to feel awfully damned foolish if he doesn't go for this, Fargo."

"He'll go for it."

"He's awfully old, Fargo."

He sat her in the chair, touching her shoulders as he adjusted her sitting position. Her flesh bedazzled him for a moment and despite the fear and tension of the night, he felt himself surge to arousal.

"You'll make him feel young again."

"Boy, do you have the gift for bullshit."

Fargo laughed. "Now remember, when he comes through that door, you make yourself look as available as possible. I only need him distracted for a few seconds."

"Then you jump him from behind the door?"

"That's how it's s'posed to work, anyway. Maybe he turns around on me and shoots me in the gut."

"Let's hope not."

"And Stephanie, as soon as the door opens, you start your fake crying."

Stephanie said, "It won't be fake, Fargo. This whole thing has really started to overwhelm me."

"Well, just remember to start crying."

Fargo tried to imagine what it would be like for Noah. You open the door and you are immediately confronted with two images. A voluptuously beautiful girl sits in a chair, her legs parted slightly, the totality of her lush body on display. Your attention is about to settle on that when—

At the same time, the gunshot-like cries of a woman in great distress can be heard from the corner. Which do you look at? What's going on here? Is this some kind of set-up? But before you can puzzle your way through all the questions, suddenly all such questions are moot. Because here comes Fargo out of nowhere—actually, from behind the door—tackling you around the neck and hurling you to the ground, taking your Spencer away from you as you see the floor coming up to smash your face in.

I sure as hell hope this works, Fargo thought. "What's he doing now?"

"Going to the bathroom."

"Peeing, I take it?"

"Yes. If it was the other one, I couldn't watch."

"I don't blame you."

"If you manage to get his Spencer away from him," Nancy said, "remember that I'm the one who gets to kill him."

"I thought you wanted to kill Burgade," Fargo said.

"Just like a man," Nancy said. "You don't listen to anything women have to say." She paused. "The deal we had, Fargo, was that I got to kill old Noah and Stephanie got to kill Burgade."

"I want to shoot him right in the crotch," Stephanie said.

"What's he doing now?" Fargo asked Stephanie.

"Taking a drink from a bottle of bourbon."

"He's getting ready," Fargo said.

133

"I still don't know how you could do that to your own brother," Stephanie said. "Now, he's checking over his Spencer."

"All right," Fargo said. "Everybody get ready."

"I have the easy part," Nancy said. "All I have to do is sit here in my birthday suit."

They got ready. Nancy sat up straight in the chair. Stephanie cleared her voice several times, so her fake weeping would come across clearly. And Fargo positioned himself behind the door. This could all go very wrong very easily, he knew. Burgade could suddenly show up again, for one thing. He'd hear the commotion and be in the cabin with his dogs instantly. At this point, he wouldn't give a damn about saving the hunt. He'd just want to protect Noah. And he'd do anything he could to save the old man, up to and including siccing his dog on the two young women and Fargo.

This time, Stephanie spoke up without being asked. "He's got a pistol in his holster. He's checking that one too. He looks like he's about ready to come down here. He's straightening his hat. He's dusting off his trousers. He's straightening his hat again."

He smiled. Kind of sweet, what she was doing. She didn't have to give him every damned tiny detail. She'd probably report him picking his nose. Lord, he hoped not.

"Here he comes," she said.

23

The closer they got to shore, the more the growl intensified in Voodoo's chest and the harder the time Burgade had restraining the dog. Voodoo had seen and smelled a man being torn apart. He wanted some of the same for himself.

Nobody on the dock. Nobody on the near shore. The river was still, shimmering silver in the moonlight. Burgade wondered if seeing Aaron Tillman die had unhinged the animal, made him start imagining things because he was so eager for the hunt. But, no. Voodoo was the best hunter Burgade had ever come across. He could track a snowman in a blizzard, as some of the older dog handlers like to say.

Voodoo ran several feet ahead. The growling grew steadily louder.

Burgade suddenly got interested in this little prowl. He was sure now that Voodoo had scented something, sure now that somebody had come onto the island. Maybe they had guessed that everybody was busy with something else and it was a good time to sneak on. But who were they and why were they here? Whoever they were, they'd done him a favor. He would have the pleasure of telling Noah that he'd been wrong. That Voodoo had correctly warned them of intruders. Burgade would also like to tell Noah how wrong he was about many other things, too. But he knew better than that.

They sure weren't good at stealth, Burgade realized soon enough. They were not far away from him as he walked the shore. Maybe ten, fifteen feet into the forest at most. But they trampled on and stumbled over everything in their way.

They'd likely heard Voodoo by now, too. Burgade sensed

this because of how they'd picked up their pace. Running now—trampling and stumbling all the way—in the direction of the clearing and the cabins.

He knew a cut-off about three-quarters of the way to the cabin. He caught up with Voodoo and stage-whispered a new command. The animal smelled of heat and spittle and urine. Its entire body shuddered and shook. It sensed Burgade's excitement. If Burgade was excited, that meant the kill was near.

Voodoo led the way into the forest. Knew instantly the origin of the trail and all its curves through the woods.

A different light spilled on the trail, a light broken by the leaves and limbs of the trees that formed a canopy above them, a grotesque cross-hatching of silhouettes slithery as snakes. A nightmare land that looked like nothing of earth at all, with the eyes of a dozen different kinds of creatures noting their passage, clinging to the undergrowth and the vast bases of ancient trees, afraid to reveal their hiding places lest Voodoo find them and eat them the way monsters in storybooks ate little children.

Voodoo no longer growled. He was smart and he was hungry. Growling would only warn the prey of his approach.

When they reached the cut-off, Burgade took the dog and they hid in a shallow ravine. Burgade could see over the top of it. It was unlikely the intruders could see him at all—or wouldn't, anyway, until it was too late.

Burgade's first sight of them genuinely shocked him. He hadn't put faces to the intruders in his mind—they'd just been people who shouldn't be here and were going to pay with their lives for being here. More fun for the dogs. Or for Noah, if he wanted to get in a little extra hunting tonight.

He hadn't been expecting Tom Tillman and Liz Turner, that was for sure.

Voodoo leapt out of the ravine. Burgade shouted for him to stop but Voodoo was beyond taking orders. At least for now.

Burgade scrambled from the ravine, his rifle ready but it was already too late.

There in the prehistoric pathways of the forest, in the

shattered, alien light of the moon, Voodoo was already in the process of killing Tom Tillman.

He had gone without pause for the man's throat, slamming him back into a tree, ripping enough out of the throat to render the man half-dead on the spot, and then, on the second pass, throwing him to the ground so that he could essentially tear the man in half vertically, feasting on the gore as he went.

"Stop him! Stop him!"

Liz Turner was beyond hysteria. She was under the panicked impression that Tom Tillman was somehow still alive. But a glance at the throat certainly told otherwise.

Burgade shouted and shouted and shouted for the dog to stop. He didn't give a damn about Tom. It was the fact that Voodoo no longer obeyed him that stunned and worried him.

And then Voodoo vaulted from the massacred corpse on the ground to Liz Turner where he repeated almost exactly the same process he'd used with Tom Tillman. He did this without warning. He did this despite the cries of Burgade to stop. He did this with a single menacing—terrifying— glance at Burgade as his body flew toward Liz. He had warned Burgade that he was no longer in control.

Burgade started running. He had no doubt that if he didn't get out of here, he would be Voodoo's next victim.

"Something's wrong," Stephanie said. "Burgade just came running back. His dog isn't with him and he looks kind of crazy."

Fargo jumped up from the chair and hurried to the caged window.

She hadn't been exaggerating. Though he couldn't hear what Burgade was saying, he could see that Burgade was violently upset about something. He stood only inches from Noah and shouted in his face. He kept pointing to the forest and waving his rifle around.

Noah started looking at the forest, too. And then Burgade must have said something that shocked Noah because Noah's expression and posture changed completely. He looked older suddenly. He hefted his Spencer and the two men returned to the same path Burgade had taken.

"What's going on, Fargo?" Stephanie said.

Nancy had put her shirt on and padded over to the window.

"Something happened in the woods," Fargo said. "Something that got to Noah pretty bad."

"You should've seen his face," Stephanie said. "He really looked sick. And old. I wonder what Burgade told him."

Fargo said, "Hurry up and get dressed."

Nancy looked confused. "What's going on?"

Fargo walked over to the west corner of the cabin and said, "Remember how you told me the roof leaked pretty bad every time it rained?"

"Uh-huh."

"Well, it could've rotted some of the cedar they used to build it. I'm going to find out in a hurry." He grabbed a chair, carried it to the west corner, climbed up on it.

Nancy said, "You mean I got undressed for nothing, Fargo?"

"Not for nothing," he smiled. "You gave me a nice, long look at a beautiful body."

She laughed as she slid into the rest of her clothes. "So you're not going to hide behind the door?"

"Not if we can get out of here before they come back."

He worked with his fist, striking the underside of the roof's corner. He got discouraged at first because he couldn't find any point that the soaking rain had weakened.

"Any luck, Fargo?" Stephanie asked.

"Not yet."

And he didn't have any luck at all, either. Not with the western corner of the roof. He jumped down, picked up the chair and raced over to the eastern end of the cabin.

He did the same thing there. Tested the underside of the roof for weak points. He was quickly discouraged.

Then his fist practically went right through the shingles and he knew he'd found the spot he was looking for. He started tearing away the roofing, pitching the rain-soaked material to the floor as he went.

When he'd created a hole big enough to crawl through, he pulled himself up and onto the roof.

"Hurry up," he said to the women.

They each gave little mews of excitement. This was the

only real opportunity for freedom they'd had since being kidnapped and brought here. They took a moment to enjoy the fact. They sounded giddy to be free of their shackles and to be headed for the roof.

Fargo knelt next to the hole on the roof, helping them climb, climb and wriggle their way up to the hole and through it. All the time watching the edge of the forest for any sight of their captors. All he could hear was the dogs. They were still some distance away, which meant that Noah and Burgade were probably still with them. He couldn't imagine that they'd let the dogs run free.

From the roof to the ground. Sweat blinded all three, pasted clothing to their flesh, added a briny smell to the air.

They ran.

"Where're we going?" Nancy said as they plunged down a path.

"I think the dock is this way," Fargo said. "I sure as hell hope so, anyway."

The clear, simple light of the moon broke into splinters on the branches overhead. The forest became an immense land of crooked trees and looming limbs and holes that could break the bones of careless runners. Not that there was any way they could slow down. Fargo became machine-like at times like these. He had only one thought. To get to the dock and whatever boat Noah had come in on. And then to escape from the island and its dogs.

Nancy was the first to fall, stumbling and smashing her knee against a tree root that had grown across the path. She tried to muffle her cry but the pain was too much. Fargo dropped back and bent to her. All he could hope was that the knee wasn't broken. He pulled her to her feet and said, "Try to stand on it."

They were both panting, chests heaving. Stephanie hovered nearby, anxious to get moving again but also fearful that her sister was badly injured.

"Try and put your weight on it," Fargo said.

She complied. But she also cried out this time with frightening ferocity. Not much doubt now. The knee was probably broken.

He grabbed her around the waist, slung her over his shoulder, and they set off again, this time at a much slower pace.

Fargo listened to the night as he made the twisted journey to the water. From what the sounds told him, the dogs had revolted. He had heard of such things. That once dogs tasted human flesh, they were no longer intimidated by the symbols of human flesh, their masters. From the shouts of both Noah and Burgade, from the snarls, growls, and cries of all four dogs, it was easy to picture what was going on. Noah and Burgade were probably holed up somewhere, holding the dogs at bay as long as they could.

The dogs would win. It might take them all night but they would win unless the two men could find a way to kill them first. Chances are they would tire and make one small, brain-weary mistake and then the dogs would take advantage of it and kill them in the most savage way possible. He wondered if the two men understood this. Probably not. They were probably under the impression that they could regain control of the situation.

And then the smell came to Fargo, the smell of the river. The heat and roll and flow of all that water in the hot moon-filled night. Frogs and flapping fish and deep running currents that would take them to freedom.

The river. The only escape.

When they came to the mouth of the path, Fargo stopped. He'd have to set Nancy down soon. Her weight, the heat, and his exhaustion were all pressing in on him.

Noah had come in a simple rowboat. It sat rolling in the pitch of the water next to the larger boat that Fargo and Aaron had been brought here in.

To his right, he could hear the barking, angry dogs, loud now, at least two of them sounded brain-addled, plagued by their own form of madness.

But still no sight of the two men.

Burgade's sharp, sudden curse revealed their position. Like Fargo, they'd realized that the only place of safety on the island was in a tree.

Four huge oak trees formed a natural wall just east of the dock. The tree roots were such that the wall was extended to the length of thirty yards. Noah and Burgade were somewhere in the farthest tree, invisible among the heavy leafage and the night.

Two of the dogs lay dead on the shore. That apparently

accounted for the increased frenzy in the enraged barks and whines and cries of the surviving animals. Pure crazed rage. They jumped and jumped and snapped at the tree where the two men hid. Somehow, they had escaped the bullets that had felled the others.

This represented another change in plans. If they went for the boats, the dogs would eat them alive. Fargo couldn't carry Nancy much farther. And finding the place where he'd originally planned to leap into the water—climb as high as he could into the trees and then vault out across the water—was too distant now. The oaks were perfect for jumping. Two problems, of course. The dogs and the men.

He told the women what he had in mind. The three of them fell back on the trail. They couldn't go anywhere near the oaks on the ground. The dogs would see them. And then there were Noah and Burgade.

Some of the trees were post oaks and dated up to 400 years. The red cedars mixed in with the oaks had been put at more than 500 years old. The trees were huge, their branches vast, their trunks and many of their limbs impenetrable.

Fargo started puzzling through the interlacing of trees, which branches led where. Two smaller oaks were set several yards behind the wall of oaks. He found one point where a couple of sturdy looking branches from the smaller trees came very near the branches of the larger trees. The trees were covered with twisted stems and many wide, heavy limbs that could easily support humans, as the Indians here had long ago discovered when a few dozen of them must have used those same trees to hide and attack settlers.

"I'm going up in this tree," he said to the women. "I'm going to do a little fast exploring. If I can find a safe perch for us, I'll haul you up, Nancy. Think you can make it on your own, Stephanie?"

"Damn right I can."

He smiled at her determination. These were two gals who put the bravery of most men to shame.

He started his climb, needing three tries to jump high enough to swing up on a branch and begin his ascent. The rough bark of the oak smelled of heat and wood. The leafage was more exotic, having a faintly spicy air. It probably wasn't the oak he was smelling. It was probably the heavy undergrowth below. God alone knew what grew there.

He was monkey-agile in the tree. He'd spent enough of his boyhood learning the secrets of trees and he'd spent enough of his young manhood getting to know the way Indians used trees for scouting posts and as the perfect vantage point to fell your enemies from. Rifle or arrow, it was up to you.

He climbed upward, slipping a few times and ripping open his knuckles in the process. After visiting upon the tree bark a full thirty second blast of cursing, he found what he was looking for—a perfect perch for them to hide in until they made their move to the oaks in front.

Now, the test. If he could get safely from one tree to the next, he would get the women up here. That would still leave the problem of how to swing out over the water. The shoreline was shallow, maybe six feet, but that could be a long ways to go when you were trying to fly over it.

He inched across the limb that jutted out, almost all the way to the other tree. It was thick and sturdy but it could be rotten at some point; he couldn't know without walking it.

Leaves slapped his face. Bugs of myriad varieties covered him. At a couple of points, the limb creaked. Fortunately, it didn't seem weak enough for his concern, just noisy. He continued on.

But how solid was the branch extending from the big oak in front? He soon found out. Holding on to a branch above him, he went hand-over-hand to the front tree. He let himself down slowly, testing the new branch with his weight. He wished he could see between the leaves and the darkness, but his hearing was his only guide. The dogs had run away from the trees—their barks came from a slightly different direction now—probably keeping themselves safe from the gunshots Noah and Burgade continued to grind out.

The branch was solid. He eased himself all the way over to the center of the giant oak, pushed back some thin branches, and got his first look at the shore from this perspective. Moonlight made everything look so tranquil.

Now, he had to get the ladies up here before the dogs came after them.

24

Noah Tillman knew there was only one way he could appease the two remaining dogs. He was too old to chase them down. And if he tried to get to his boat, they'd grab him for sure.

He needed to give them a distraction. A distraction as good as Aaron had been. While they were in the course of dining on human meat, they'd be oblivious to all else around them. What was required was more human meat.

Burgade was wasting his shots. But the very act of shooting seemed to reassure him that he was in control of the situation.

The first two dogs, Noah himself had killed. And that, to be fair, had been easy because all four had collected at the base of the tree. He'd simply fired downward, giving the two dogs behind the opportunity to flee.

Those dogs were now silken shadows with the bloodied teeth of sated wolves, slipping in and out of moonlight, never standing still for even ten seconds at a time. It was clear that in their way they knew damned well what had happened and damned well what was planned for them. They wanted vengeance, owing it to their fallen fellows. And they wanted human meat.

Noah noticed it first, the turbulence in the vast oak tree down the way, the tree on the edge that helped form the natural wall on the shallow shore. Huge branches shook their leaves, the very air—sticky and still this far up—was violated by what appeared to be a terrible battle between night creatures that threatened to bring part of the tree down.

But Noah knew better. There were no nightbirds nor

night animals this far up that could cause this kind of turmoil within the interconnected trees. No animal but the human animal. And that animal could only be Fargo.

Noah knew that he should have killed him right back at the cabin and that trying to hunt him was a mistake. You didn't hunt a man like Fargo. Not if you were sensible. You set your pride aside and did what was prudent and expedient. You killed him the first chance you had. He should have taken the extra minute—he should have denied himself the fantasy of stalking Fargo in this forest—he should have pumped three or four bullets from his Spencer right into Fargo's head.

Now Fargo was up in the trees and was no doubt planning to attack Noah and Burgade. A man like Fargo didn't need a gun to make a kill. Not in these circumstances. He could make his way through the trees and attack at will with stones. He seemed to be damned handy with stones.

For the first time in years, Noah Tillman felt trapped. None of his power, none of his money was worth a damn up here.

"What's that?" Burgade said, noticing how the trees near the top were suddenly moving, something having invaded them.

"Keep your damned voice down."

"What's going on?" Burgade said in a quiet voice.

"What do you think's going on? That sonofabitch Fargo knows we're up here and he's come after us."

"He doesn't have a gun."

"I'd still put my money on him."

"Don't worry," Burgade said in his best tough voice. "I can handle it."

No need to repeat that Burgade was a fool. He was such a fool that he couldn't even understand the trap they were in. Now they had two enemies at their heels. And Burgade was oblivious to each.

"In fact, I'll take care of that sonofabitch right now," Burgade said without any warning.

And then he went berserk, firing round after round into the general area that had trembled moments ago with Fargo's passage.

He kept firing and firing until Noah, going berserk in his own way, grabbed Burgade's rifle and snatched it from him.

Burgade was haunched down on a broad limb that was a straight drop to the ground far below. There were a few slender fingers of branches but nothing that would break a man's fall. What would break such a fall was the ground itself and it would break many other things besides—the skull, the back, the pelvis, the legs.

And then the dogs would close in.

Noah Tillman was as hungry to push Burgade to his death as the dogs were to eat him. He stared at the stupid gunny with rage burning his gaze and his heart pounding hard.

Soon, Burgade, soon.

It took twenty of the sweatiest minutes of his life for Fargo to get the women in position on the broad tree limb that overlooked that shallow shoreline.

By now it was clear that Nancy's knee had been shattered. She did an amazing job of swallowing her pain.

Fargo spent ten minutes trying to assess where they would land if they got lucky in jumping off the limb. He calculated it four different times to see if there was any way to improve their chances. There wasn't. The limb was sturdy for about six feet. It then began to taper off. The length of the entire branch was maybe ten feet, its tip close enough to let a person get lucky if he got a good leap. But the useful, safe part of the wide branch ended at about six feet, meaning that even with a good leap they would land in the shallowest part of the water. They might not even reach the water, smash themselves up on the sand. And the dogs would have at them.

If they couldn't reach the water then they would have to get to Burgade's boat and stow away there. Once aboard, they could shut the doors to keep the dogs from getting at them.

If they didn't injure themselves so badly in the jump that they couldn't move.

If the dogs didn't attack them instantly.

If Noah and Burgade didn't open fire on them as soon as they landed.

But there was no way he was going to risk the lives of the ladies. He'd already made up his mind to that. This perch near the top of the tree sure wasn't ideal but at least the dogs couldn't get at them. The women could survive here for some time if they needed to.

There was also, he'd come to realize since doing his calculations, no way that he could dive or jump from this limb. He was simply too high up. Even landing in the water would probably break a couple of ribs if he landed flat. He would need to climb back down the tree a few inches at a time, the same way he'd come up.

He told the ladies his plan. They listened, sitting where the branch grew from the huge oak. Stephanie had seated Nancy so that she could elevate her leg, providing her with only slight relief from the constant pain.

"I'm being selfish here, Fargo," Stephanie said. "But what if the dogs get you? Or Burgade shoots you? How're we ever going to get down from here? We could starve to death. Those dogs could be on this island a long time. There're plenty of animals to eat."

Nancy was the sentimental one. "Hell, Fargo, I'm worried about *you*. My sister's a very nice girl but she's a little self-centered. You're taking a big risk down there on the ground."

"The only hope we've got is to get our hands on some guns," Fargo said. "Kill the dogs and then kill Noah and Burgade if we have to."

"I know," Nancy said. "But the burden's all on you."

"I didn't mean to sound so cold, Fargo," Stephanie said. "I'm sorry."

"You were just telling the truth. I may not make it down there. But right now I'm the only chance we've got. If the dogs or Burgade get me, you'll have to do the best you can."

The first rifle shot spanged off the bole of the tree about eight inches above Fargo's head. Three more shots followed quickly. The women ducked, Fargo dove for the branch and clung to it.

Pieces of bark, leaves, even some nuts stored there by squirrels began falling on their heads. The shots had been way wide of their mark but they'd done considerable damage to the tree.

"That's all we need," Stephanie said bitterly.

"Now we need a gun more than ever," Fargo said. "I'll have to kill Noah and Burgade right along with the dogs."

"They might be able to see you climbing down the tree," Nancy said.

"I still have to do it, Nancy. I'll try to find a way down the far side of the tree. It's so wide I doubt they can pick me off 'til I get close to the bottom. And from there I can drop to the ground."

"And run into the dogs," she said.

"Well, I know I sound selfish again, but we can't just sit here and do nothing, Sister. One of us has do something to get us to freedom. And Fargo's chances are better than ours."

Fargo nodded.

Talk was through. What mattered now was trying to find a firearm or two.

Fargo began his descent.

Noah was already planning what he would tell people when he got back to town. There would be too many questions—and questioners—for him to play the aloof land baron role he was accustomed to.

Fargo, Burgade, and the sisters would be no trouble. A mass grave right here on the island would take care of them.

The other two, Liz and Tom—they would take some explaining. But that was where Fargo would be the proper villain. Tom found him raping Liz. Fargo killed both of them and then dumped their bodies out on the island where Noah's dogs savaged them. Noah would be forced—for the first time—to admit that he *had* dogs like these. But that would help him look like the good citizen. He was so afraid of keeping the dogs anywhere near town that he put them on the island.

As for Fargo, Noah would insist that he'd escaped. And then offer a huge reward for his capture. He would claim that Aaron was missing, too, and that he believed Fargo had likewise killed him and buried the body somewhere.

His final act would be to burn down everything on the island and keep it off-limits to the town, posting a guard to make sure the ban was enforced.

"You even listening to me, Noah?" Burgade said.

"What?" He knew that he sounded old and a bit confused. He had rarely been forced to explain himself to anybody. This story he had to concoct needed to cover so many things, would it satisfy people? Or would all the people who envied and hated him see this as the first serious opportunity to bring him down?

All these deaths tonight, it was supposed to have been a night of hunting, of the singular pleasure of stalking and killing the most challenging prey of all, your own species. Now, all he could think about was going back to the estate and getting a good night's sleep, safe and comfortable in the knowledge that he was Noah Tillman by God and nobody could touch him.

"I was saying that I think the dogs are hiding. They know we'll kill them if they come out in the open. So they're playing hide-and-seek with us. They won't show themselves until we go back down."

Noah snorted. "You give them a hell of a lot of credit. You sound like they can think the way humans do."

Burgade defended his two remaining dogs. "We've trained them to hunt and kill, Noah, that's all they know. They can use more of their senses, that's what makes them so dangerous."

"Right now, I'm more worried about what Fargo's up to."

"Maybe all those shots—maybe I killed him."

Noah refrained from tearing into Burgade. Good as Burgade was in some ways, he always tried to convince himself that everything would be fine. Noah knew better. For things to be fine—for things to go your way—you had to manipulate everything from behind the curtain, like a puppeteer. You couldn't count on killing a man by pounding fifteen shots into a leafy hiding place a good ways away.

"He's alive," Noah said.

"What makes you think so?"

"What makes you think he's dead?"

"All those bullets—he must've—"

"Did you hear him fall out of the tree?"

"Well, no, I guess not."

"Did you hear him scream?"

"No."

"Then assume he's alive. And that he's coming for us."

"I can handle him."

"Oh, sure, Burgade. We're sitting up in a tree with two

insane animals waiting to rip us apart. And we've got the Trailsman trying to figure out how to kill us." He spat. "Yes, it really sounds like you've got things under control."

Burgade was a sulker and he started sulking now. He was sick of this rich old bastard always challenging him, questioning him. If Burgade was such a know-nothing then why had Noah hired him in the first place? And if Burgade was such a know-nothing, how was it that he'd run the island so efficiently and effectively all these years?

Nobody had ever snuck on for long. Burgade took care of them. Noah had said that he wanted the most vicious dogs a man could train. And Burgade had trained them just that way. So well, in fact, that they were now hiding from the animals.

And Noah was trying to make himself feel better at Burgade's expense. But Burgade was sick of being berated, scorned, made fun of by this old bastard.

Burgade leaned out over the sturdy branch they sat on, stared down at the ground.

The thought came out of nowhere. If the dogs were hiding, waiting for them to leave the tree, what if he pushed Noah off the branch. What if Noah became his decoy?

While the dogs were feasting on the old man's body, Burgade would have enough time to sneak away to the boat—and escape from the island.

He looked at the old man in a whole new way, smiling at Noah as he did so.

Noah wasn't a human being—he was a big, juicy side of beef.

Just the kind those dogs had dreams about.

Fargo made his descent into a darkness as complete as the inside of a coffin. This side of the tree was angled in such a way that moonlight did not reach it. The interwoven branches from other trees also hampered his climb down. He had to forage through leafage as thick as bushes in some places. He also had to find branches that worked as handholds and ladder rungs for his feet. They weren't always readily available.

The work was slow. During the descent, he had to worry about falling from the tree and breaking his bones. While crashing probably wouldn't be all that bad, that wouldn't help him with the dogs. The dogs would likely be on him in seconds.

He slipped twice and damned near slid down several feet of rough-barked tree. Another time a branch his hands clung to snapped. Luckily, his feet found a solid, if slender, branch a few feet below. The tree was far too wide to wrap his hands around but while he slipped down those few feet, he hugged the tree the way he would hug a grizzly he was wrestling—he never let go of the damned thing.

Darkness. Sweat. Barked knuckles, scraped palms. Awareness of the waiting beasts. Awareness that Burgade and Noah could start firing again at any time.

Then there was the snake. Someday this would make a great story to be told over whiskey in a saloon. But at the moment it happened, nothing at all was funny about it.

As his feet touched a sturdy branch below, he automatically reached up to reposition his hands on the branch he presently held. But in repositioning them, he accidentally moved them over about a foot, taking a moment to flex them. They were badly cramped from the descent.

If there had been any light, he would have known better because he would have seen the snake. At least an outline of it. And so he would have put his hands back where they'd been and quickly dropped down to the next branch, keeping an eye on the creature so that it didn't, in its spitting anger, dive down for it.

The furious rattling noise it made, just as it was about to strike, startled Fargo so much, he jerked his hands from the branch and crouched down instinctively. This, in turn, caused him to fall backward and crash down through heavy leafage. He might have gone all the way to the ground if he hadn't reached out blindly and grabbed a handful of leaves and fragile tiny branches that stopped his fall. He swung like an ape from this spot, better than forty feet from the ground, until his feet, desperately searching for a perch, found a gnarled knot of stunted branch that allowed him to hug the tree and stand erect.

He once again pressed himself to the tree. Closed his eyes. Let his hot, ragged breathing find its natural rhythm and pace.

He gave himself a few minutes to put his mind and body

back together and then began his descent into utter darkness again. This time, he moved more cautiously.

The closer he got to the ground, the more keenly he listened for the dogs. He began to peer around the tree, holding on with one hand, using the other to part leaves for a look at the shore. Burgade's boat, traced by moonlight, looked like a means of holy deliverance straight out of the holy book itself. If he could only get to that, find a weapon aboard. . . .

When he was ten feet from the ground, he stopped and listened as intently as he could. He could hear, faintly, the voices of Noah and Burgade—not the exact words—but he certainly heard the urgency of what they were saying. They had to know that if Fargo got a weapon, the first thing he would do once he got past the dogs—*if* he got past the dogs, of course—was to come after them.

What he didn't hear was any evidence of the dogs. Just those voices and all the surrounding clamor and clutter of the animals, large and small, dangerous and docile, that inhabited the forest.

He spent five long minutes listening to the night and the woods. Now, he had no other choice but to try to reach Burgade's boat.

He wondered which would attack him first. The dogs or Noah and Burgade. These were the times he had to consciously hold his fear at bay and work on pure instinct.

He eased himself down the remaining circle of tree. Dropping to the ground would make too much noise.

One foot had barely touched the sandy soil when he heard the scream.

It would have been funny if they'd been mind readers. They both had the same idea. Noah would push Burgade's ass out of the tree, the dogs would attack him and give Noah cover to reach the boat and safety. Not the row boat. Those damned dogs would jump in the water to get him. He needed a cabin where he could lock himself in as he was pulling away from the shore.

Burgade's plan varied only slightly. He planned to push Noah out of the tree, wait for the dogs to attack him and then shoot the dogs while they were beginning their meal. If Fargo had a weapon of any kind, he would have used it by now. And that meant that Burgade, with Noah and the dogs dead, could easily stroll to the boat, get it ready for sailing and push off. He could feel a southeasterly wind starting to build now. He could be in Little Rock in under two days.

They sat and watched each other.

Noah thought: he gets leg cramps about every ten minutes. Then he stands up. Next time he stands up, I'm going to push him right off this branch. Just take my Spencer and shove him right in the crotch to get him off-balance, and then give him another poke of the Spencer and knock him all the way down. He'll be dead when he hits the ground. Or he'll wish he was.

Burgade thought: so what I do is get up real gentle, like I've just got another cramp or somethin', and then when I get on my feet I just kick out and knock him right off this branch. He'll be dead when he hits the ground. Or he'll wish he was.

They eyed each other some more and continued to assess each other, refining their plans all the while—just a bit here, a bit there—and then they talked and waited to fill the time. Noah waited for Burgade while Burgade waited for some instinct to tell him that this was the exact right moment to stand up and give a boot-shove to old Noah, sending him to certain death.

"Legs," Burgade said.

"Huh?"

"Legs. Cramps."

"Oh."

Here we go, Burgade thought.

Here we go, Noah thought.

And that was when it happened. If either of them had known a damned thing about the stress two full-grown bodies put on a tree branch the size of the one they were cohabiting at the moment, they would have listened carefully to the faint creaking, the faint cracking the branch made from time to time.

Burgade leaned back against the trunk of the tree, ready to lunge suddenly and push the old man off his perch.

Noah hefted his Spencer, pretending to be examining it

out of sheer admiration, but ready of course to plow its butt right straight into Burgade's crotch and send him shouting and cursing to his death, his well-deserved death.

The moment was upon them, now.

Both ready to betray and murder the other.

And then it happened.

All those tiny creaks and cracks.

All that weight on this one branch.

A scream.

Fargo's first impression was that only one man was screaming.

Then it became obvious that it came from the both of them.

By the time he realized this, he heard their bone-crushing landing on the ground. And then something remarkable happened—or didn't happen. No dogs appeared. No dogs barked. No dogs even whimpered.

Something was wrong here.

Fargo edged his way from behind the tree to the narrow shoreline. In the distance, he could see two prone human bodies lying in the moonlight. One of them—Burgade, it appeared—was carefully raising and moving his right arm. Noah didn't move at all.

Here was his chance for a weapon. He couldn't move directly on Burgade. Even injured, the man could kill him. Fargo would have to move through the forest and come up behind him.

Fargo slipped back into the darkness of the woods. He wondered what the ladies were making of all this. Screams. The hard landing. And now the strange silence.

He found a narrow trail, partly obscured by undergrowth that took him all the way to the last of the oaks that formed the natural screen and wall along the shoreline.

He had to be as quiet as possible. Burgade might have a broken bone or two but all his other faculties could still be running. He might have even heard him already, but there was no time to worry about the danger ahead. Fargo wanted a weapon and Fargo wanted off the island.

He stumbled only once, on a tree root he couldn't see, pitching head first into a small patch of bramble that put several good scratches on his arm. A moment of sheer frustration—all these traps he had to overcome before he set this island to rights. Sometimes even the Trailsman got discouraged.

But then he found an opening to go through—one that held nothing more problematic than a few long ferns that wanted to cool and soothe and heal his body. At least, that was what it felt like after all the bramble.

Burgade wasn't waiting for him. Burgade lay flat on his face. His rifle was four feet from his hand where, apparently, it had fallen. No sign of movement from Noah, either. His Spencer wasn't close at hand, but scattered in pieces several feet away.

Either one of them could wake up and turn on him.

He crept up to Burgade, his eyes scanning up and down the body, looking for any sign of life. Sometime between the time Burgade had raised his arm to see if it was broken and now, he'd fallen down the long, dark well into unconsciousness.

Fargo felt a moment of pure, unreasoning, unadulterated joy. This was easy. He'd just walk over and pick up Burgade's gun. If the dogs did show up—exactly where the hell were they anyway—he'd be prepared.

He *did* love dogs. But he'd have no trouble killing these two. Burgade had trained all the canine virtues and beauty out of them. Now they were nothing more than enemies.

He started walking toward the rifle. And then he heard the growl. He scanned the shore and then the edge of the timber. Where were they? Nearby, from the sound of their low, trembling growls. And another question. Why weren't they attacking?

He reached instinctively for his Colt but it wasn't there. He felt as if his hand had been amputated, he was so used to his Colt riding on his hip, ready at all times when needed. He moved even faster now. He was just picking up Burgade's rifle, just thinking that everything was in hand again, when he heard a voice that sounded as if it was coming from the realm of death.

In his rush to get Burgade's rifle, Fargo had forgotten all about Noah. While Fargo sensed that Burgade had passed on, Noah had rallied enough to dig his pistol from its holster while sitting up on one elbow. Awkward as his position was, he could shoot just fine. "You just stay there with your hands in the air, Fargo. What the hell did you do with my dogs is what I want to know?!"

"I was wondering about them myself." He couldn't help himself; he just kept staring at Burgade's rifle. His mind, as well as his eyes, was fixed on it.

Fargo took a slow step forward.

"One more and you're dead," Noah grunted.

"It's all over for you, Noah."

"Maybe, maybe not. But you try for that rifle and I'll be glad to take you with me, Fargo."

"Burgade may still be alive. You want me to check his pulse?"

"I want him dead. Now you just stand there and watch."

It was something to see. For all the pain he must have been in after his fall, for all his age, for all his general infirmities, Noah found the same strength now that he'd found when he was recreating this section of country in his own image. There were only a few men like him on the entire planet. Some of them used their vision and intelligence and savvy for good and created new medicines and new laws and new businesses. And some used their gifts for bad. Like old Noah here.

He kept his gun on Fargo all the time he was getting to his feet. Twice he looked as if he would fall over. His gun hand was shaky. He winced in pain. His knees trembled. But somehow he managed to stand strong and purposeful.

"I'm getting on the boat there and you're going to push me out in the water."

"That's a good-sized boat."

"I could still do it myself if I had to. You're a tough man, Fargo. It won't be easy but I know you've got it in you. And anyway, you won't have much choice. If you don't do it, I'll kill you on the spot. Sound reasonable?"

Fargo chose silence once again.

"You go ahead of me down to the dock, Fargo."

Fargo shrugged. There had to be a way of escape now. Maybe the water. Yes, the water. Dive deep and long. Swim wide. Come up on another part of the island and get the girls down from the tree. Then make a final run on Noah.

Noah was a mind reader. "The water'll tempt you. But you won't make it, Fargo. Now you get down there to that boat."

He took two steps and heard it then. Heard it again. The low rumble. The dogs.

This time, he knew exactly where it came from. The cabin of the boat. The dogs were in there. Hard to know why they'd elected to hide in there. Maybe it was as simple as getting away from the gunfire that had felled the other two. That explained why they hadn't attacked him or Burgade or Noah.

Noah was still several feet behind him. Apparently he hadn't heard the dogs. Noah's hearing wasn't good enough to pick up their rumble.

When Noah reached the boat, Fargo stood aside so that Noah could walk up the plank stretching from the dock to the deck.

Noah said, "You know what you need to do."

Fargo nodded. All he could hope was that the dogs would remain quiet enough to fool Noah.

Noah got on the plank and said, "For right now, you stand about halfway to Burgade then you come back down here when I tell you to."

"Why?"

"Because I don't move as fast as you do and you'll try to jump me when I'm on the plank. Now get up there. I'll pull up the plank and you push me out away from the dock."

He didn't have any choice, anyway, so he agreed.

As he walked toward the dead body of Burgade, he realized that here was a chance to get a weapon. If he could act fast enough. If things played his way. Noah still didn't seem to know that the dogs were hiding in the boat's cabin.

"That's far enough," Noah shouted.

The plank was wide enough that he had room to turn around on it if he needed to. He could easily look back at Fargo if he needed to. And kill him if he needed to.

And then it happened.

Happened with such speed and fury that Fargo could only sort it all out later.

When Noah reached the boat itself, he shouted for Fargo to walk up to the shoreline and give the craft the push it needed to get into the water. With the strong wind, Noah would have no trouble getting away.

Fargo looked longingly over his shoulder at Burgade's

rifle. The temptation was strong to lurch to the side and dive for it. But Noah's marksmanship was pretty damned good. Plans always looked so easy in the abstract. He'd just fade back and grab Burgade's rifle and. . . .

He had no choice but to oblige Noah.

He started across the narrow band of sand separating him from the boat and that was when the world ended for old Noah.

While he was holding his pistol on Fargo, he reached around and opened the cabin door and finally figured out— far too late—where the dogs had been hiding all along.

A lot of it happened in shadow and a lot of it happened below the top edge of the boat's sheer, making it impossible for Fargo to see anything.

But he heard plenty.

Noah shrieking, Noah sobbing, Noah crying out for help to the vast indifferent universe, and finally Noah screaming as the dogs dined and supped on his flesh and blood, rending and gnawing him down, as they did to the others.

He heard all this on the run, as he rushed back to Burgade's rifle. He knew that it wouldn't be long before the dogs came for him. They'd hidden after the deaths of their fellows but now that they'd toppled and consumed Noah, they were eager for more human food.

He killed the first one when it came lurching over the top of the boat's sheer. It took two bullets to its chest in midflight. It seemed to hang there for a moment so long it was as if the very earth itself had stopped moving. And then it collapsed, dead, to the ground.

The next dog came right behind it but this one hit the ground and moved so fast that Fargo had some difficulty finding it in the shadows. It was just about to leap at him— it probably couldn't have covered the eight or nine feet that separated them but it was sure willing to give it a try—when Fargo found a true shot and blasted the animal, exploding the top of its head into several flying pieces.

There was a certain melancholy for Fargo in killing these animals. By nature they would have been good and loyal companions. But Burgade had perverted their nature. It was almost too bad that they hadn't been able to have the pleasure of ripping him apart, too.

*　　*　　*

Fargo and the women watched the sunrise from the bow of the boat. It was a lavish spectacle, streaks of red and aqua lending rare colors to the dawn. A faint fog on the water gave the limestone cliffs on either shore a feel of long-ago times before even the Indians were here. Fargo felt a reverence for untrammeled land such as this. It was in the wilds that he felt the greatest peace.

"I hope I get to spend a little time with you before you go," Nancy said, sliding her hand through Fargo's as he watched the far dock begin to sketch itself into reality behind the fog.

"Don't forget about me," Stephanie said.

Difficult to do, Fargo smiled, as she pressed her bountiful breasts against his arm. "I don't think you have to worry about that."

"In fact," Nancy said, "we were talking about maybe getting a room next to yours in a hotel, you know, while everything gets sorted out."

"Yeah, Skye, what do you think of that?"

"Well, there sure will be a lot to sort out." And there would be. With Noah, Tom, and Aaron dead, somebody would have to take over not only the estate, but the town—introduce it to real democracy and say goodbye to what had been virtual one-man rule.

"You didn't answer my question," Stephanie said. "What about the idea of staying in adjoining hotel rooms, Skye?"

He laughed and drew them both to him. The sun wasn't the only thing rising at this moment. "I've sure heard a lot worse ideas in my day," Skye Fargo said. "I sure enough have."

LOOKING FORWARD!

**The following is the opening
section of the next novel in the exciting
Trailsman series from Signet:**

THE TRAILSMAN #264
Snake River Ruins

*Washington Territory, early 1861—
Where the promise of a new life
reaped horrible death.*

The big man in buckskins did not know what to make of
it. Rising in the stirrups, he studied the stretch of dirt road
ahead. His piercing lake-blue eyes flicked from the wagon
that sat in the middle of the road to the woodland on either
side. Something wasn't right.

Skye Fargo slid his right hand to the Colt on his hip. He
had survived as long as he had by always heeding his instincts, and they were telling him he must proceed with
caution. He clucked to the Ovaro and rode on at a slow
walk, alert for anything out of the ordinary. All seemed as
it should be except that he didn't hear any birds. Usually,
where there were a lot of trees, there would be sparrows
and robins and jays and ravens, yet the woods were
deathly still.

The wagon was a one-horse farm wagon, common on the

frontier, with a bed nine feet long, a high seat at the front, and large wooden hubs. What it didn't have was the farmer who owned it or a horse to pull it. Apparently, it had been abandoned. Which begged the question: why?

Dismounting, Fargo checked the wheels and the springs and the tongue. They were in working order. Nothing was broken. It made no sense for the owner to have left the wagon sitting there. Even stranger, part of the harness was still attached. Squatting, Fargo examined it. The harness had been cut.

The tracks were plain enough for a seasoned tracker to read, and Fargo was one of the best. The tracks told him the farmer had jumped down from the seat, cut the horse loose, climbed onto it, and galloped off to the west. All of which spelled trouble. The farmer had needed to get out of there in a hurry or he would never have cut expensive harness. Someone or something had spooked him.

Fargo made a circuit of the wagon. His first guess was hostiles, although to his knowledge none of the local tribes were acting up. His second guess was outlaws, but that seemed even less likely. The Palouse River country of southeastern Washington Territory held little to attract the lawless breed. He found no other recent prints, nothing that would explain the mystery.

Baffled, Fargo forked leather and lifted his reins. A crudely painted sign five miles back had pointed him in the direction of a settlement called Carn, where he intended to buy coffee and sugar and a few other items he was running low on, and push on.

The region consisted of gently rolling hills broken by isolated buttes and scattered tracts of woodland. It was sparsely populated but Fargo imagined that would change in a few years as word of its rich soil spread. He would be sorry to see that happen. There were already too many people flocking west.

Fargo couldn't explain it, but suddenly he felt overrun by uneasiness. Having learned to trust his instincts, he twisted in the saddle but saw nothing to account for it. His hand on his Colt, he gigged the pinto stallion north. He was almost clear of the trees when movement in the brush caused him to rein up again. He caught a flash of greyish-brown. Something had been there but now it was gone. After a minute he trotted into the open.

The heat hit him like a physical force. It was an exceptionally hot summer, with daytime temperatures well above one hundred degrees and nighttime temperature dipping only to the mid-eighties. Drought had the land in a stranglehold. Streams that normally ran year-round had dried up. Springs that had always been reliable were bone dry. Were it not for the Palouse River to the north and the Snake River to the south, there wouldn't be a drop of water to be had anywhere.

Fargo's canteen was almost empty, yet another reason to visit Carn. The settlement was bound to have water. Or so he hoped. It wasn't uncommon for droughts as severe as this one to wither whole communities and leave ghost towns in their wake.

The vegetation was in dire need of rain. All the grass was brown and brittle. The trees drooped like ranks of old men about to keel into their graves, their branches bent, their leaves the same color as the baked earth.

Pulling his hat brim low against the harsh glare of the burning sun, Fargo mopped at his forehead with the sleeve of his buckskin shirt. He was caked with sweat. His mouth was dry, his throat parched, but he resisted the temptation to take a sip from his canteen. He could wait until he reached Carn.

The settlement was new. Fargo knew nothing about it but imagined it was no different from countless others he had come across in his travels. The road wound over a low hill and when he came to the crest he spotted a large animal, lying on its side, west of the road. He rode over to see what it was.

As Fargo approached, a swarm of flies rose thick into the air. The stench was awful. He had found a dead cow. Staying well away, he circled it. The cause of death wasn't readily obvious. It might have died of thirst. It might have been killed by a mountain lion or a bear. The eyes and throat were gone. So was its soft underbelly and hindquarters. Coyote prints placed the blame for the missing parts on scavengers.

Fargo continued north. One dead cow in and of itself was not unusual. But in another mile he came on a second, and soon after, a third. Both were in the same state of decomposition. He wondered if maybe an outbreak of disease was to blame.

Carn lay nestled in a broad valley at the base of the hills. From a slope half a mile away, Fargo counted two dozen buildings. Most flanked the town's lone street. Holding to a walk, he soon came to a house that stood off by itself. A stone fence bordered a neatly trimmed yard. Once a flower bed had flourished, but now the flowers were dead, their petals shriveled like burnt leaves.

Fargo was almost past the fence when he spotted a dead dog. It lay on its side, its tongue jutting from its mouth, its eyes glazed. The cause of death was hard to tell. There wasn't a mark on it. The mouth crawled with flies. Plainly, it had been dead for several days.

Puzzled as to why its owner hadn't buried it, Fargo glanced at the house. A rocking chair lay overturned on the porch, and the front door hung open. He drew rein and cupped a hand to his mouth. "Anyone home?"

No one answered.

After dismounting, Fargo walked to the gate. It was ajar wide enough for him to step on through and then along a cobblestone walk to the porch. "Is anyone here?" Silence mocked him. He knocked but no one came to the door. Poking his head inside, he saw a coat stand on the hall floor. On the wall beside it was a smear of blood.

Palming his Colt, Fargo entered. The parlor was in shambles. Most of the furniture had been thrown violently about, and a chair cushion had been torn apart. He checked all the downstairs rooms but none of the others had been disturbed. As he climbed the stairs a familiar stench wreathed him, and he untied his red bandanna from around his neck and retied it over his nose and mouth.

He thought he would find another dead dog, or maybe a cat. The first two bedrooms were empty, but the door to the third was closed. Pushing it open, he nearly gagged at the odor. On the bed lay the source, an elderly man, fully clothed, a peaceful smile on his wrinkled face. The top of his head had been blown off. Beside him lay a shotgun.

Fargo closed the door and went outside. He sucked in long breaths to clear his lungs and paused at the gate. He was unsure what to make of it all. Why had the old man been left there like that? Hadn't anyone noticed something was amiss?

The Ovaro had its ears pricked and was staring toward the settlement a hundred yards away. Fargo looked but saw no one. Possibly the heat had driven them indoors. But that did not explain the absence of horses at the hitch rails, nor the absence of all sound.

"I don't like this," Fargo said to the pinto as he stepped into the stirrups. Halfway between the house and the outskirts lay a rotting cat. Farther on next to a dry horse trough, was another dead dog. "What the hell is going on?"

Fargo rode down the center of the street searching for inhabitants. No one appeared in any of the doorways or windows. Nor did he hear a single human voice. It was as if all the people had up and vanished.

Fargo had been in ghost towns before. Many a boomtown had gone bust, forcing the people to go elsewhere to earn a livelihood. But this was different. He had a feeling of foreboding, a sense that something was gravely wrong and he should light a shuck while he still could.

At the hitch rail in front of the general store, Fargo reined in. He slid down, shucked his Henry rifle from the saddle scabbard, levered a round into the chamber, and stepped onto the plank boardwalk. "Anyone here?" he called out. Again silence taunted him. He tried the latch and the door swung in on well oiled hinges. The interior was stifling hot.

His spurs jangling, Fargo moved down the center aisle. The store was clean and tidy. The shelves were fully stocked with everything from dry goods to tools to bolts of cloth for making dresses. A birdcage hung from a low beam but the cage was empty, its tiny door open. He came to the counter and ran a finger across it. There was no dust.

Which meant that whoever owned it had not been gone for long.

Coffee, tea, and sugar were on a shelf behind the counter. Fargo was about to help himself when he decided to check the rest of the town. There might be a perfectly logical explanation for the missing settlers. Maybe they were having a town meeting. Or maybe they were attending a funeral. He went back out.

The Ovaro's head was drooping, its eyes half closed. Fargo wished there were some shade handy, but he did not intend to stay long. He peered into building after building, but they were all the same. At the end of the street stood the stable, its double doors wide open. Across from it was a freshly painted church with a tall steeple. Just as he set his eyes on it, the bell in the belfry clanged.

Fargo smiled to himself. So that was where they were. Rather than interrupt their services, he crossed to the saloon and pushed on the batwing doors. As saloons went, it had little to recommend it. A few tables, a dozen bottles of liquor, and a painting above the bar of a plump woman in a full-length dress. In a corner sat a piano. No one was there, which was mildly surprising. Most towns, no matter how small, had their share of folks who wouldn't set foot in God's house if they were paid to. And the saloon was where they spent most of their time.

Shrugging, Fargo walked behind the bar and helped himself to a bottle of coffin varnish. It wasn't the best but it washed the dust from his throat and put a knot of warmth in his stomach. Not that he needed to be any warmer. The windows were shut and it had to be one hundred and ten degrees in there, if not more.

After selecting a table, Fargo sat with his back to a wall and filled a glass. He drank slowly, hoping the church service or whatever it was would end soon and he could get on with his business and get out of there. But after twenty minutes he grew impatient and walked into the street.

Not a sign of life was to be seen. No dogs, no cats, no pigs wandering aimlessly or chickens scratching in the dust. He unwound the Ovaro's reins from the hitch rail and made for the stable. The trough in front was bone dry. He

164

walked the stallion inside and received another surprise. The stalls were empty. Every last one. But if the horses weren't there, where were they?

Even with the doors open the stable was a furnace. Fargo led the Ovaro back out and over to a trough near the church. It, too, was dry. But there had to be water there somewhere.

The church bell clanged again.

Fargo decided enough was enough. He strode up to the door and opened it. A gust of hot air fanned his face as he removed his hat and entered. It took a few seconds for his eyes to adjust, and when he did, he couldn't believe what he was seeing. No one was there. The church was as deserted as the rest of the town.

The bell clanged, and Fargo hurried past the pews to a small door to the belfry. He opened it, and wished he hadn't. An abominable reek filled his nose before he could think to hold his breath. His stomach churned, spewing bitter bile into his throat. Covering his mouth with his hand, he backed out. The reek followed, clinging like invisible mist.

The image of what Fargo had seen was seared into his brain; the bell far overhead, a rope suspended from it, and suspended from the rope, the parson. A noose had dug deep into the minister's neck, and his face was swollen and discolored. From the grisly look of things, he had been hanging there a couple of days, if not longer.

Anxious for a breath of untainted air, Fargo hurried out and leaned on the rail. To the growing mysteries was added another: had the parson been hung, or had he hung himself? Regardless of which it was, why had the good people of Carn left the man there to rot? The more Fargo found, the less sense it made.

"Where is everyone?" Fargo shouted; and when he received no reply, he smacked the rail in frustration.

The Ovaro was staring down the street again, its ears pricked as before. Fargo stepped past it but saw nothing. "Damn it. There has to be someone around." Pointing the Henry at the ground, he banged off a shot. The slug kicked up dirt, but that was all it did. No one appeared. No doors or windows were flung open. No shouts were raised.

That was when the full grim truth hit him: Fargo realized he must be the only living person in Carn. Everyone else was either gone—or dead. But why? And where to? An epidemic wasn't to blame. Not unless it was an illness that made people hang themselves and put guns to their own heads.

Fargo had a sudden urge to get out of there. To put as many miles as he could between himself and Carn. He shoved the Henry into its scabbard, climbed onto the pinto, and reined south. He had no personal stake in whatever was going on here. When he reached Fort Boise he would report what he had found. Let the army deal with it.

The *clomp* of the stallion's heavy hooves seemed unnaturally loud. Fargo came to the general store and stopped. He had come this far; he might as well get what he came for. Quickly, he swung down. "I'll be right back." He took a step, then whirled.

Across the street a door slammed.

Every nerve taut, Fargo listened. He thought he heard footsteps but he couldn't be sure. He scanned every window, every doorway. If someone was there, why hadn't they shown themselves? he asked himself.

More eager than ever to light a shuck, Fargo piled coffee, sugar, matches, and ammunition on the counter. He left enough money to cover the cost and scooped everything into his arms. Another minute, and it was all in his saddlebags and he was on his way. *Good riddance,* he thought.

Fargo was not going to look back, but as he passed the last building, he did. And involuntarily stiffened. A face was watching him from a second-floor window. It was a young girl, as pale as snow, stringy bangs hanging to her eyebrows. "I'll be damned!" he blurted, and smiled and waved. The girl melted into the murk behind her.

Fargo never hesitated. In a twinkling he was off the Ovaro. The door was locked but he did not let that stop him. Lowering his shoulder, he stepped back, then slammed into it hard enough to splinter the wood and tear it off one of its hinges. He was in a feed and grain store. Farm implements were everywhere.

To Fargo's left were stairs. He took them three at a bound. At the top he paused to get his bearings. The window the child had been at was in a room on the right. "Little girl?" He barreled on in. It was a storeroom for sacks of seed piled almost to the ceiling. He had to thread through them to reach the window. The room had not been dusted in ages, and there in the dust under the window were small footprints. He hadn't been seeing things.

"Girl, where are you? I won't hurt you." Fargo checked the storeroom and had just stepped into the hall when a crash downstairs brought him to the stairs in a rush. A shadow flitted across the front window. He raced down and on out into the glare of the sun. Blinking, he looked both ways, but the girl, if indeed she had been responsible, was gone.

Fargo gazed south. In half an hour he could reach the main trail. By the end of the day he could be halfway to the border. Instead, he went into the middle of the street and tried again. "Girl? Where are you?" He didn't expect her to answer, and she didn't disappoint him.

Suddenly Fargo heard a soft sound behind him. Thinking it must be her, he smiled and turned, saying, "I meant what I said about not hurting you. All I want—" His voice died in his throat.

No other series has this much historical action!

THE TRAILSMAN

Available wherever books are sold, or
to order call: 1-800-788-6262